The Sturdy Oak

THE STURDY OAK

A Composite Novel of American Politics

The chapters collected and (very cautiously) edited by
ELIZABETH JORDAN

With an Introduction by Ida H. Washington

OHIO UNIVERSITY PRESS
ATHENS

First published by P. F. Collier & Son and Henry Holt and Company in 1917.
Ohio University Press paperback edition 1998
Introduction © 1998 by Ida H. Washington
Ohio University Press, Athens, Ohio 45701
Printed in the United States of America

02 01 00 99 98   5 4 3 2 1

Illustrations by Henry Raleigh

Library of Congress Cataloging-in-Publication Data

The sturdy oak : a composite novel of American politics / the chapters
collected and (very cautiously) edited by Elizabeth Jordan : with an
introduction by Ida H. Washington.
    p.   cm.
  ISBN 0-8214-1200-0 (pbk. : alk. paper)
    1. New York (State)—Politics and government—Fiction.   2. Women—
Suffrage—New York (State)—Fiction.   3. Satire, American.
  I. Jordan, Elizabeth Garver, 1867–1947.
PS3500.A1S78   1998   99-11258
813'.52—dc21   CIP

Contents

ILLUSTRATIONS

INTRODUCTION

"We have only lost a battle, not the war!" Carrie Chapman Catt exhorted weary workers for the cause of woman suffrage at campaign headquarters on election night in 1915. The discouraging results of a referendum vote on woman suffrage in New York State had just come in. Undaunted, and with banners held high, the defeated suffragists marched out into the city streets to speak to homeward-bound crowds emerging from the theaters. Two days later an overflow gathering in Cooper Union pledged $115,000 to a renewed campaign. By New York law two years had to pass before the referendum could again be brought to the voters, but the suffragists lost no time in rallying support from every possible source. It was as a part of this second New York campaign that *The Sturdy Oak* was planned and written.

The war for woman suffrage in America had raged for sixty-seven years, ever since the first convention "to discuss the social, civil and religious rights of woman" at Seneca Falls, New York, in 1848. From that time on, women had battered away constantly at state and national legislative doors, first to get the question of enfranchisement put before the voters, and then to win support for the right of women to vote.

The first success came in the far west when, in 1869, the Territory of Wyoming gave the same voting rights to women as to men. But by 1915 only eleven states had granted women full suffrage, and these were all "new" states west of the Mississippi. In the older and more conservative eastern states little progress had been made. At the national level, bills introducing suffrage amendments had been introduced repeatedly—and repeatedly they had been ridiculed and killed in committee. When the "Anthony Amendment" finally came to a vote for the first time in the House of Representatives in 1915, it was soundly defeated.

The 1915 effort to win support for woman suffrage from the voters of New York was the largest and best-organized campaign

held in any state. Two hundred thousand campaign workers were
recruited and trained to carry the message into every home and
place of work in the state. In addition the suffragists sponsored parades and picnics, sporting events and theater productions—any
affair that could bring their cause before a crowd of voters. They
topped off their campaign with the largest parade ever seen in
New York City, as forty thousand women marched up Fifth Avenue
from early in the morning until long after dark. When the ballots
were counted, however, woman suffrage lost by almost 195,000
votes.

In the spring of 1916, as the workers for woman suffrage were
laying plans for another attack on the bastions of male supremacy,
the idea for *The Sturdy Oak* was born. Serious argument had been
tried, and would be used again, but other means had to be found to
undermine the long-established prejudice against allowing women
into the voting booths. One alternative was narrative fiction.

The storyteller's art is a time-honored vehicle for messages that
are hard to deliver directly. With the magic power of words the nar-
rator transports the reader into the experiences of fictional characters to share their anxieties, laughter, and tears. In the story world
the reader lives a second life, and returns to everyday surroundings
enriched by the fictional experience.

The Sturdy Oak follows the rules of an old parlor game. One
person began the narrative, another continued it, another followed,
each contributing one chapter to the whole. A new element was
introduced into the game pattern by providing a list of characters
and plot outline before the narration commenced, so that each
writer worked within an established framework. Another unusual
aspect of the book is that it was written gratuitously in support of
a political cause: the authors donated their work and all profits
from serial publication to the campaign for woman suffrage. *The
Sturdy Oak* appeared in serial form during the autumn campaign of
1917, with book publication in November of that year.

Two years earlier the powerful Tammany Hall political machine in New York City had opposed the suffrage referendum, and
conservative forces in upstate New York had joined to complete
the defeat of the measure. By 1917, however, pressure to give

women the vote was growing throughout the nation, and in New York as well. Wives of prominent industrialists and politicians had joined the ranks of the suffragists, among them the wives of Tammany bosses. In 1917 Tammany workers received a new message: "Hands off! Let the voters decide as they please." The resulting vote for the suffrage referendum in New York State was a critical turning point in the national campaign. The leaders of the suffragists had realized for some time that winning the most populous state was essential to establishment of national woman suffrage. The passage of the nineteenth amendment to the United States Constitution was still three years in the future, but Carrie Chapman Catt hailed the New York victory with the words: "The victory is not New York's alone. It's the nation's. The 66th Congress is sure to pass our federal amendment."

There is much in *The Sturdy Oak* that reflects the New York campaign of 1915–17. The setting is the fictional city of Whitewater in upstate New York, the type of conservative industrial community least open to social change. Idealistic reformers in Whitewater are pitted against a ruthless political machine, and the traditional image of man as "the sturdy oak" supporting woman, "the clinging vine," is ridiculed in the portrayal of an engaging young couple, George and Genevieve Remington. Nonetheless, the purpose of the book is not primarily ridicule, but reform, and the reader is taken through the steps by which a confirmed anti-suffragist is gradually transformed into a supporter of the suffrage cause. The characters are for the most part surprisingly alive and believable despite their clearly polemic purpose in the narrative, and real comedy enlivens even the most contrived and least credible situations.

Two of the group who produced *The Sturdy Oak,* Elizabeth Jordan and Mary Heaton Vorse, had participated in the writing of another composite novel, *The Whole Family* (1908). For this earlier book, each of a dozen authors, including William Dean Howells and Henry James, had been assigned one character to portray, providing together a picture of a family and its close associates.

ELIZABETH JORDAN (1865–1947), who coordinated the work of the five men and nine women writers of *The Sturdy Oak,* began her journalistic career in her native Milwaukee, then moved to

New York to serve on the staff of the *World*. There she attracted attention for her human interest stories about the mountain people of Virginia and Tennessee, followed by a series of fictionalized accounts of inmates of local jails and asylums. In 1893 she reported the trial of Lizzie Borden and subsequently used that experience as the basis for a very popular short story, "Ruth Herrick's Assignment." From 1900 to 1918 she served as editor of *Harper's Bazar* (the spelling changed to *Bazaar* in 1929), while she continued to write fiction to augment her income. She also collaborated with Anna Shaw in the writing of the suffrage leader's autobiography, *The Story of a Pioneer* (1915).

MARY AUSTIN (1866–1934), who set the theme for the story and also contributed chapter 13, became known for her articles and stories about the American Southwest, its natural phenomena and its people. In 1912, however, after her novel *A Woman of Genius* appeared, she began to spend more time in New York and became actively involved in the woman suffrage movement.

The opening chapter of *The Sturdy Oak* was written by SAMUEL MERWIN (1874–1936). He was an editor of *Success Magazine* from 1905 to 1911 and the author of numerous historical and social problem novels. Three of these were co-authored by HENRY KITCHELL WEBSTER (1875–1932), another writer of historical fiction and the contributor of chapter 6. HARRY LEON WILSON (1867–1939), who supplied chapter 2, served as editor of *Puck* from 1896 to 1902 and was the author of western tales, including *Ruggles of Red Gap* (1915). The author of chapter 3, FANNIE HURST (1889–1968), at twenty-six years of age was the youngest member of the group. She was an indefatigable worker for social reform and used her considerable gifts as a writer and speaker to protest injustice wherever she found it. Social and economic discrimination against women was a favorite theme of her fiction, but at the writing of *The Sturdy Oak* she was only beginning her long career. DOROTHY CANFIELD (1879–1958), the next author in the sequence, was already a widely published writer of short stories when her early novels *The Squirrel-Cage* (1912) and *The Bent Twig* (1915) voiced a protest against the exclusion of women from useful participation in the world's work. Following her chapter is one by KATHLEEN NORRIS (1880–1966), who had been a journalist before embarking on a prolific literary career that saw the production of eighty-one novels, as well as numerous short stories and articles. ANNE O'HAGAN (1869–1934), who wrote chapter 7, was a reporter and editor for the New York *World* and *Journal* from 1892 to 1897 before she turned to freelance writing of fiction, articles, and verse. The next author, MARY HEATON VORSE (1874–1966), lived a double literary life as a journalist of social reform and an author of romantic fiction. Her journalism reflected a lifelong commitment to the cause of labor justice, especially for women and children, while the romances that flowed from her pen were a necessary source of income for herself and her three children. A born rebel, she bitterly resented the restrictions of house and motherhood, much preferring the excitement of the strike line and the newspaper office. ALICE DUER MILLER (1874–1942), the author of chapter 9, became a best-selling writer in 1916 with her book *Come out of the Kitchen,* which had appeared serially in *Harper's Bazar* the year before. From 1914 to 1917 she had a column in the *New York Tribune* entitled "Are Women People?" Chapter 10 is the work of ETHEL WATTS MUMFORD (1878–1940), the author of satirical books and plays and copublisher of *The Complete Cynic's Calendar.* Then comes a chapter by MARJORIE BENTON COOKE (1876–1920), an accomplished monologist who began writing fiction in 1899 and also created dramatic sketches. WILLIAM ALLEN WHITE (1868–1944), the author of chapter 12, was the owner and editor of the *Emporia (Kansas) Gazette.* His editorials were reprinted in newspapers across the country and involved him in national political activities. He also authored books of fiction and nonfiction, including biographies of the presidents Theodore Roosevelt and Calvin Coolidge. LEROY SCOTT (1875–1929), who wrote the concluding chapter of *The Sturdy Oak,* was a newspaperman and author active in settlement work in New York. He served as assistant editor of the *Woman's Home Companion* from 1900 to 1901.

The prominent illustrator Henry Raleigh provided drawings of scenes from the novel. A westerner, born in Oregon and educated in California, he had come to New York where he did illustrations for *the Saturday Evening Post* and *Cosmopolitan* magazines.

Is *The Sturdy Oak* still relevant today? Have the questions raised by the novel been answered and the problems solved? The particular political issue that lies at the center of the plot, the enfranchisement of women, has long been settled—or has it? Women not only vote, but are even found in high political office. But did giving women the vote promote them automatically to the equal partnership demanded by the novel? Did it guarantee an equal sharing of responsibilities in the home, or equal opportunity and recompense in the workplace? Or even freedom from harassment in any sphere of life?

Thanks to laws passed in the ensuing decades (though still unevenly enforced), once-powerless women now have some recourse to legal action. But despite new legislation, many of the social problems raised in *The Sturdy Oak* refuse to go away. Workers who disagree with their employers or resist their advances still put their jobs in jeopardy; wives who disagree with their husbands still suffer psychological or even physical abuse. Women who of necessity work long hours still face the double fears of loss of income and failure as mothers. We meet the type characters of the novel and the situations they encounter with few changes in our daily news today.

Political campaigns today are perhaps cleaner than the one depicted in *The Sturdy Oak,* but it is a big perhaps. Money and control, which play an important role in the novel, are issues still current. Dishonesty and violence as roads to power bring fresh accusations. The contrast of wealth and poverty, of privilege and deprivation, presented as problems without real solutions in the novel, are still problems that resist solutions in the cities of America today.

Although this was not intended as a muck-raking novel, it reflects in many ways the need for exposure and reform of social ills, a literary and journalistic tendency that has pervaded twentieth-century writing. We can note with regret, and even alarm, the continued relevance of issues raised by *The Sturdy Oak:* slum conditions and the additional problems when those slums are wiped out by the gentrification of poor housing areas, labor laws that hurt as much as they help the workers, pollution, health care, mob violence, and influence peddling.

Beyond the social and political content, the collection of episodes by skilled writers presents a fascinating study in comparative literary styles. Realism and romanticism, descriptive, dramatic, and narrative passages rub shoulders. Only remarkably skillful editing has brought this diversity into a cohesive whole and smoothed the seams between the parts. For a teacher of writing, this book could be a valuable text. So often it is necessary to focus on what is bad in writing, but here fourteen successful practitioners of the art of storytelling show the many ways of successfully treating the same theme. What a wonderful array of examples for a beginning writer who is still seeking a personal style!

A search among the writers of *The Sturdy Oak* for the characteristics of the composite author behind the composite novel reveals more than a common commitment to the cause of woman suffrage. All except the precocious Fannie Hurst were between the ages of thirty-five and fifty, well established in careers that usually included journalistic writing in support of social reform. Their presentation of character and action has the sure touch of authors who know how to stir and hold the interest of their readers. Because of their skill, even eight decades after its publication *The Sturdy Oak* is still, as a reviewer for the *New York Times* said in 1917, "irresistibly readable."

"Nobody ever means that a woman really can't get along without a man's protection, because look at the women who do."

Preface

At a certain committee meeting held in the spring of 1916, it was agreed that fourteen leading American authors, known to be extremely generous as well as gifted, should be asked to write a composite novel.

As I was not present at this particular meeting, it was unanimously and joyously decided by those who were present that I should attend to the trivial details of getting this novel together.

It appeared that all I had to do was:

First, to persuade each of the busy authors on the list to write a chapter of the novel.

Second, to keep steadily on their trails from the moment they promised their chapters until they turned them in.

Third, to have the novel finished and published serially during the autumn Campaign of 1917.

The carrying out of these requirements has not been the childish diversion it may have seemed. Splendid team work, however, has made success possible.

Every author represented, every worker on the team, has gratuitously contributed his or her services; and every dollar realized by the serial and book publication of "The Sturdy Oak" will be devoted to the Suffrage Cause. But the novel itself is first of all a very human story of American life today. It neither unduly nor unfairly emphasizes the question of equal suffrage, and it should appeal to all lovers of good fiction.

Therefore, pausing only to wipe the beads of perspiration from our brows, we urge every one to buy this book!

ELIZABETH JORDAN

NEW YORK,
November, 1917.

PRINCIPAL CHARACTERS

George Remington. . . . Aged twenty-six; newly married. Recently returned to his home town, New York State, to take up the practice of law. Politically ambitious, a candidate for District Attorney. Opposed to woman suffrage.

Genevieve. . . . His wife, aged twenty-three, graduate of Smith. Devoted to George; her ideal being to share his every thought.

Betty Sheridan. . . . A friend of Genevieve. Very pretty; one of the first families, well-to-do but in search of economic independence. Working as stenographer in George's office; an ardent Suffragist.

Penfield Evans. . . . Otherwise "Penny," George's partner, in love with Betty. Neutral on the subject of Suffrage.

Alys Brewster-Smith. . . . Cousin of George, once removed; thirty-three, a married woman by profession, but temporarily widowed. Anti-suffragist. One Angel Child aged five.

Martin Jaffry. . . . Uncle to George, bachelor of uncertain age and certain income. The widow's destined prey.

Cousin Emelene. . . . On Genevieve's side. Between thirty-five and forty, a born spinster but clinging to the hope of marriage as the only career for women. Has a small and decreasing income. Affectedly feminine and genuinely incompetent.

Mrs. Harvey Herrington. . . . President of the Woman's Club, the Municipal League, Suffrage Society leader, wealthy, cultured and possessing a sense of humor.

Percival Pauncefoot Sheridan. . . . Betty's brother, fifteen, commonly called Pudge. Pink, pudgy, sensitive; always imposed upon, always grouchy and too good-natured to assert himself.

E. Eliot. . . . Real estate agent (added in Chapter VI by Henry Kitchell Webster).

Benjamin Doolittle. . . . A leader of his party, and somewhat careless where he leads it. (Added in Anne O'Hagan's Chapter).

Patrick Noonan. . . . A follower of Doolittle.

Time. . . . The Present.

Place. . . . Whitewater, N.Y. A manufacturing town of from ten to fifteen thousand inhabitants.

I

BY SAMUEL MERWIN

GENEVIEVE REMINGTON had been called beautiful. She was tall, with brown eyes and a fine spun mass of golden-brown hair. She had a gentle smile, that disclosed white, even teeth. Her voice was not unmusical. She was twenty-three years old and possessed a husband who, though only twenty-six, had already shown such strength of character and such aptitude at the criminal branch of the law that he was now a candidate for the post of district attorney on the regular Republican ticket.

The popular impression was that he would be elected hands down. His address on Alexander Hamilton at the Union League Club banquet at Hamilton City, twenty-five miles from White-water (with which smaller city we are concerned in this narrative), had been reprinted in full in the Hamilton City *Tribune;* and Mrs. Brewster-Smith reported that former Congressman Hancock had compared it, not unfavorably, with certain public utterances of the Honorable Elihu Root.

George Remington was an inch more than six feet tall, with sturdy shoulders, a chin that gave every indication of stubborn strength, a frank smile, and a warm, strong handclasp. He was connected by blood (as well as by marriage) with five of the eight best families in Whitewater. Mr. Martin Jaffry, George's uncle and sole inheritor of the great Jaffry estate (and a bachelor), was known to favor his candidacy; was supposed, indeed, to be a large contributor to the Remington campaign fund. In fact, George Remington was a lucky young man, a coming young man.

George and Genevieve had been married five weeks; this was their first day as master and mistress of the old Remington place on Sheridan Road.

Genevieve, that afternoon, was in the long living-room, trying out various arrangements of the flowers that had been sent in. There were a great many flowers. Most of them came from admirers of George. The Young Men's Republican Club, for one item, had sent eight dozen roses. But Genevieve, still a-thrill with the magic of her five-weeks-long honeymoon, tremulously happy in the cumulative proof that her husband was the noblest, strongest, bravest man alive, felt only joy in his popularity.

As his wife she shared his triumphs. "For better or worse, for richer or poorer, in sickness and health . . ." the ancient phrases repeated themselves so many times in her softly confused thought, as she moved about among the flowers, that they finally took on a rhythm—

> "For better or worse,
> For richer or poorer,
> For richer or poorer,
> For better or worse—"

On this day her life was beginning. She had given herself irrevocably into the hands of this man. She would live only in him. Her life would find expression only through his. His strong, trained mind would be her guide, his sturdy courage her strength. He would build for them both, for the twain that were one.

She caught up one red rose, winked the moisture from her eyes, and gazed—rapt, lips parted, color high—out at the close-clipped lawn behind the privet hedge. The afternoon would soon be waning—in another hour or so. She must not disturb him now.

In an hour, say, she would run up the stairs and tap at his door. And he would come out, clasp her in his big arms, and she would stand on the tips of her toes and kiss away the wrinkles between his brows, and they would walk on the lawn and talk about themselves and the miracle of their love.

The clock on the mantel struck three. She pouted; turned and stared at it. "Well," she told herself, "I'll wait until half-past four."

The doorbell rang.

Genevieve's color faded. The slim hand that held the rose trembled a very little. Her first caller!

She decided that it would be best not to talk about George. Not one word about George! Her feelings were her secret—and his.

Marie ushered in two ladies. One, who rushed forward with outstretched hand, was a curiously vital-appearing creature in black—plainly a widow—hardly more than thirty-two or thirty-three, fresh of skin, rather prominent as to eyeballs, yet, everything considered, a handsome woman. This was Alys Brewster-Smith. The other, shorter, slighter, several years older, a faded, smiling, tremulously hopeful spinster, was Genevieve's own cousin, Emelene Brand.

"It's so nice of you to come—" Genevieve began timidly, only to be swept aside by the superior aggressiveness and the stronger voice of Mrs. Brewster-Smith.

"*My dear!* Isn't it perfectly delightful to see you actually mistress of this wonderful old home. And"—her slightly prominent eyes swiftly took in furniture, pictures, rugs, flowers,—"how wonderfully you have managed to give the old place your own tone!"

"Nothing has been changed," murmured Genevieve, a thought bewildered.

"Nothing, my dear, but yourself! I am *so* looking forward to a good talk with you. Emelene and I were speaking of that only this noon. And I can't tell you how sorry I am that our first call has to be on a miserable political matter. Tell me, dear, is that wonderful husband of yours at home?"

"Why—yes. But I am not to disturb him."

"Ah, shut away in his den?

Genevieve nodded.

"It's a very important paper he has to write. It has to be done now, before he is drawn into the whirl of campaign work."

"Of course! Of course! But I'm afraid the campaign is whirling already. I will tell you what brought us, my dear. You know of course that Mrs. Harvey Herrington has come out for suffrage—thrown in her whole personal weight and, no doubt, her money. I can't understand it—with her home, and her husband—going into the mire of politics. But that is what she has done. And Grace Hatfield called up not ten minutes ago to say that she has just led a delegation of ladies up to your husband's office. Think of it—to his office! The first day! . . . Well, Emelene, it is some consolation that they won't find him there."

"He isn't going to the office today," said Genevieve. "But what can they want of him?"

"To get him to declare for suffrage, my dear."

"Oh—I'm sure he wouldn't do that!"

"Are you, my dear? Are you *sure?*"

"Well—"

"He has told you his views, of course?"

Genevieve knit her brows. "Why, yes—of course, we've talked about things—"

"My dear, of course he is *against suffrage.*"

"Oh yes, of course. I'm sure he is. Though, you see, I would no more think of intruding in George's business affairs than he would think of intruding in my household duties."

"Naturally, Genevieve. And very sweet and dear of you! But I'm sure you will see how very important this is. Here we are, right at the beginning of his campaign. Those vulgar women are going to hound him. They've begun already. As our committee wrote him last week, it is vitally important that he should declare himself unequivocally at once."

"Oh, yes," murmured Genevieve, "of course. I can see that."

The doors swung open. A thin little man of forty to fifty stood there, a dry but good-humored man, with many wrinkles about his quizzical blue eyes, and sandy hair at the sides and back of an otherwise bald head. He was smartly dressed in a homespun Norfolk suit. He waved a cap of homespun in greeting.

"Afternoon, ladies! Genevieve, a bachelor's admiration and respect! I hope that boy George has got sense enough to be proud of you. But they haven't at that age. They're all for themselves."

"Oh no, Uncle Martin," cried Genevieve, "George is the most generous—"

Mr. Martin Jaffry flicked his cap. "All right. All right! He is." And slowly retreated.

Mrs. Brewster-Smith, an eager light in her eyes, moved part way across the room. "But we can't let you run away like this, Mr.

Jaffry. Do sit down and tell us about the work you are doing at the Country Club. Is it to be bowling alley *and* swimming pool—"

"Bowling alley *and* swimming pool, yes. Tell me, chick, might a humble constituent speak to the great man?"

Genevieve hesitated. "I'm sure he'd love to see *you*, Uncle Martin. But he *did* say—"

"Not to be disturbed by *any*body, eh?"

"Yes, Uncle Martin. It's a very important statement he has to prepare before—"

"Good day, then. You look fine in the old house, chick!"

Mr. Jaffry donned his cap of homespun, ran down the steps and out the front walk, hopped into his eight-cylinder roadster, and was off down the street in a second. There was a sharp decisiveness about his exit, and about the sudden speed of his machine; all duly noted by Mrs. Brewster-Smith, who had gone so far as to move down the room to the front window and watch the performance with narrowed eyes.

The Jaffry Building stands at the southwest corner of Fountain Square. It boasts six stories, mosaic flooring in the halls, and the only passenger elevator in Whitewater. The ground floor was given over to Humphrey's drug store; and most of Humphrey's drug store was given over to the immense marble soda fountain and the dozen or more wire-legged tables and the two or three dozen wire chairs that served to accommodate the late afternoon and evening crowd.

At the moment the fountain had but one patron—a remarkably fat boy of, perhaps, fifteen, with plump checks and drooping mouth. . . . The row of windows across the second floor front of the building, above Humphrey's, bore, each, the legend—*Remington and Evans, Attorneys at Law.*

The fat boy was Percival Sheridan, otherwise Pudge. His sister, Betty Sheridan, worked in the law offices directly overhead and possessed a heart of stone.

Betty was rich, at least in the eyes of Pudge. For more than a year (Betty was twenty-two) she had enjoyed a private income. Pudge definitely knew this. She had money to buy out the soda fountain. But her character, thought Pudge, might be summed up in the statement that she worked when she didn't have to (people talked about this; even to him!) and flatly refused to give her brother money for soda.

As if a little soda ever hurt anybody. She took it herself, often enough. Within five minutes he had laid the matter before her—up in that solemn office, where they made you feel so uncomfortable. She had said: "Pudge Sheridan, you're killing yourself! Not one cent more for wrecking your stomach!"

She had called him "Pudge." For months he had been reminding her that his name was Percival. And he wasn't wrecking his stomach. That was silly talk. He had eaten but two nut sundaes and a chocolate frappé since luncheon. It wasn't soda and candy that made him so fat. Some folks just were fat, and some folks were thin. That was all there was *to* it!

Pudge himself would have a private income when he was twenty-one. Six years off . . . and Billy Simmons in his white apron, was waiting now, on the other side of the marble counter, for his order—and grinning as he waited. Six years! Why, Pudge would be a man then—too old for nut sundaes and chocolate frappés, too far gone down the sober slope of life to enjoy anything!

Pudge wriggled nervously, locked his feet around behind the legs of the high stool, rubbed a fat forefinger on the edge of the counter, and watched the finger intently with gloomy eyes.

"Well, what'll it be, Pudge?" This from Billy Simmons.

"My name ain't Pudge."

"Very good, Mister Sheridan. What'll it be?"

"One of those chocolate marshmallow nut sundaes, I guess, if—if—"

"If what, Mister Sheridan?"

"—if, oh well, just charge it."

Billy Simmons paused in the act of reaching for a sundae glass. The smile left his face.

Pudge, though he did not once look up from that absorbing little operation with the fat forefinger, felt this pause and knew that Billy's grin had gone; and his own mouth drooped and drooped. It was a tense moment.

"You see, Pudge," Billy began in some embarrassment, only to conclude rather sharply, "I'll have to ask Mr. Humphrey. Your sister said we weren't—"

"Oh, well!" sighed Pudge. Getting down from the stool he waddled slowly out of the store.

It was no use going up against old Humphrey. He had tried that. He went as far as the fire-plug, close to the corner, and sank down upon it. Everybody was against him. He would sit here awhile and think it over. Perhaps he could figure out some way of breaking through the conspiracy. Then Mr. Martin Jaffry drove up to the curb and he had to move his legs. Mr. Jaffry said, "Hello, Pudge," too. It was all deeply annoying.

Meantime, during the past half-hour, the law offices of Remington and Evans were not lacking in the sense of life and activity. Things began moving when Penny Evans (christened Penfield) came back from lunch. He wore an air—Betty Sheridan noted, from her typewriter desk within the rail—of determination. His nod toward herself was distinctly brusque; a new quality which gave her a moment's thought. And then when he had hung up his hat and was walking past her to his own private office, he indulged in a faint, fleeting grin.

Betty considered him. She had known Penny Evans as long as she could remember knowing anybody; and she had never seen him look quite as he looked this afternoon.

The buzzer sounded. It was absurd, of course; nobody else in the office. He could have spoken—you could hear almost every sound over the seven-foot partitions.

She rose, waited an instant to insure perfect composure, smoothed down her trim shirtwaist, pushed back a straying wisp of her naturally wavy hair, picked up her notebook and three sharp pencils, and went quietly into his office.

He sat there at his flat desk—his blond brows knit, his mouth firm, a light of eager good humor in his blue eyes.

"Take this," he said . . .

Betty seated herself opposite him, and was instantly ready for work.

". . . Memorandum. From rentals—the old Evans property on Ash Street, the two houses on Wilson Avenue South, and the factory lease in the South Extension, a total of slightly over $3600.

"New paragraph. From investments in bonds, railway and municipal, an average the last four years of $2800.

"New paragraph. From law practice, last year, over $4500. Will be considerably more this year. Total—"

"New paragraph?"

"No. Continue. Total, $10,900. This year will be close to $12,000. Don't you think that's a reasonably good showing for an unencumbered man of twenty-seven?"

"Dictation—that last?"

"No, personal query, Penny to Betty."

"Yes, then, it is very good. You want this in memorandum form. Any carbons?"

"One carbon—in the form of a diamond—gift from Penny to Betty."

Miss Sheridan settled back in her chair, tapped her pretty mouth with her pencil, and surveyed the blond young man. Her eyes were blue—frank, capable eyes.

"Penny, I like my work here—"

"I should hope so—"

"And I don't want to give it up."

"Then don't."

"I shall have to, Penny, if you don't stop breaking your word. It was a definite agreement, you know. You were not to propose to me, on any working day, before seven P.M. This is a proposal of course—"

"Yes, of course, but I've just—"

"That makes twice this month, then, that you've broken the agreement. Now I can go on and put my mind on my work, if you'll let me. Otherwise, I shall have to get a job where they *will* let me."

"But, Betty, I've just this noon sat down and figured up where I stand. It has frightened me a little. I didn't realize I was taking in more than ten thousand a year. And all of a sudden it struck me that I've been an imbecile to wait, or make any agreement—"

"Then you broke it deliberately?"

"Absolutely. Betty—no fooling now; I'm in earnest—"

Studying him, she saw that he was intensely in earnest.

"You see, child, I've tried to be patient because I know how you were brought up, what you're used to. Why, I wouldn't dream of asking you to be my wife unless I could feel pretty sure of being able to give you the comforts you've always had and ought to have. But hang it, Betty, I *can* do it right! I can give you a home that's worthy of you. Any time! This year, even!"

"Penny, do you think I care what your income is—for one minute?"

"Why—why—"

"When I'm earning twenty dollars a week myself and prouder of it than—"

"But that's absurd, Betty—for you to be working—as a stenographer, of all things! A girl with your looks and your gifts and all that's back of you."

"You mean that I should make marriage my profession?"

"Well—well—"

"Probably that's why we keep missing each other, Penny. I've pinned my flag to the principle of economic independence. You're looking for a girl who will marry for a living. There are lots of them. Pretty, attractive girls, too. Your difficulty is, you want that sort. You really believe all girls are that sort at heart, and you think my independence a fad—something I shall get over. Don't you, now?"

"Well, I'll confess I can't see it as the normal thing. Yes, I believe—I hope—you will get over it."

"Well—" Miss Sheridan slammed her book shut and stood up— "I won't."

She stepped to the door.

"And the agreement stands. I want to keep on working. And I want to keep on being fond of you. That agreement is necessary to both desires."

She opened the door, hesitated and a hint of mischief flashed across her face. "I'll tell you just the person for you, Penny. Really. Marriage is her profession. She's very experienced. Temporarily out of a job—Alys Brewster-Smith."

He snatched a carnation from the glass on his desk and threw it at her. It struck a closed door.

The outer door opened just then, and Mr. Martin Jaffry

stepped in. He nodded, with his little quizzical smile, to the composed young woman who stood within the railing.

"Anybody here, Betty?"

A slight movement of her prettily poised head indicated the door marked "Mr. Evans." And she said, "Penny's there."

"Is he shut up, too? His partner is too important to be seen today."

"Oh no," Betty replied, inscrutably sober, "he's not important."

Mr. Jaffry wrinkled up his eyes, chuckled softly, then stepped to the door of the unimportant one. Before opening it, he turned.

"Mrs. Harvey Herrington been in?"

"Twice with a committee."

"Any idea what she wanted?"

Betty was aware that the whimsical and roundabout Mr. Jaffry knew everything about everybody in Whitewater. She was further aware that he had, undoubtedly, reasons of his own for questioning her. He was always asking questions, anyway. Worse than a Chinaman. And for some reason—perhaps because he was Martin Jaffry—you always answered his questions.

"Yes," said Betty. "She wants to pledge him to suffrage."

"Umm! Yes, I see! You wouldn't be against that yourself, would you?"

"Naturally not. I'm secretary of the Second Ward Suffrage Club."

"Umm! Yes, yes!" With which illuminating comment, Mr. Jaffry tapped on Penny Evans' door, opened it and entered.

"Spare a minute?" he inquired.

"Sure," said Penny; "two, ten! Take a chair."

"No," replied Mr. Jaffry, "I won't take a chair. Think better on my feet. I'm in a bit of a quandary. Suppose you tell me what this important paper is that George is drawing up. Do you know?"

"I do."

"Is he coming out against suffrage?"

"Flatly."

"Umm!" Mr. Jaffry flicked his cap about. "I want to see George. He mustn't do that."

"Say, Mr. Jaffry, you haven't swung over—"

"Not at all. It's tactics. I ought to see him."

"Why not run out to his house—"

"Just been there. Ran away. Some one there I'm afraid of."

"Telephone?"

Mr. Jaffry shook his head and lowered his voice.

"With Betty hearing it at this end, and the committee from the Antis sitting it out down there—the telephone's on the stair landing—"

He pursed his lips, waved his cap slowly to and fro and observed it with a whimsical expression on his sandy face, then glanced out of the window. He stepped closer, looking sharply down. A very fat boy with pink cheeks and a downcast expression was sitting on a fire-plug. Mr. Jaffry leaned out.

"Pudge," he called, "come up here a minute."

On the Remington and Evans stationery he penciled a note, which he sealed. Then he scribbled another—to Mrs. George Remington, asking her to hand George the inclosure the moment he appeared from his work. The two he slipped into a large envelope. The very fat boy stood before him.

"Want to make a quarter, Pudge? Take this letter, right now, to Mrs. George Remington. Give it to her personally. It's the old Remington place, you know."

He felt in his change pocket. It was empty. He hesitated, turned to Evans, then, reconsidering, produced a dollar bill from another pocket and gave it to the boy.

"Now run," he said.

The boy, speechless, turned and moved out of the office. His sister spoke to him, but he did not turn his head. He rolled down the stairs to the street, stood a moment in front of Humphrey's, drew a sudden breath that was almost a gasp, waddled into the store, advanced directly on the soda fountain, and with a blazing red face and angrily triumphant eyes confronted Billy Simmons.

"I'll take a chocolate marshmallow nut sundae," he said. "And you needn't be stingy with the marshmallow, either!"

At ten minutes past four, the anxious Antis in the Remington living-room heard the candidate for district attorney running down the stairs, and even Mrs. Brewster-Smith was hushed. The candidate stopped, however, on the landing. They heard him lift the telephone receiver. He called a number. Then—

"*Sentinel* office? . . . Mr. Ledbetter, please. . . . Hello, Ledbetter! Remington speaking. I have that statement ready. Will you send a man around? . . . Yes, right away. And I wish you'd put it on the wires. Display it just as prominently as you can, won't you? . . . Thanks. That's fine! Good-by."

He ran back upstairs.

But shortly he appeared, wearing the distrait, exalted expression of the genius who has just passed through the creative act. He looked very tall and strong as he stood before the mantel, receiving the congratulations of Mrs. Brewster-Smith and the timid admiration of Cousin Emelene. His few words were well chosen and were uttered with dignity.

"And now, dear Mr. Remington, I'm sure I don't need to ask you if you are taking the right stand on suffrage." This from Mrs. Brewster-Smith.

The candidate smiled tolerantly.

"If unequivocal opposition is 'right'—"

"Oh, you dear man! I was sure we could count on you. Isn't it splendid, Genevieve!"

The reporters came.

It was a busy evening for the young couple. There were relatives for dinner. Other relatives and an old friend or two came later. Throughout, George wore that quietly exalted expression, and carried himself with the new dignity.

To the adoring Genevieve his chin had never appeared so long and strong, his thought had never seemed so elevated, his quiet self-respect had never been so commanding. He was no longer merely her George, he was now a public figure. Soon he would be district attorney; then, very likely, Governor; then—well, Senator; and finally it was possible—some one had to be—President of the United States. He had begun, this day, by making a great decision, by stepping boldly out on principle, on moral principle, and announcing himself a defender of the home, of the right.

At midnight, the last guest departed. George and Genevieve stepped out into the summer moonlight and strolled arm in arm down the walk.

Waddling up the street appeared a very fat boy.

"Why, Pudge," cried Genevieve, "what on earth are you doing out at this time of night!"

"I'm going home, I tell you!" muttered the boy, on the defensive. He carried a large bag of what seemed to be chocolate creams, from which he was eating.

As he passed, a twinge of memory disturbed him. He fumbled in his pockets.

"I was to give you this," he said then; and leaving a crumpled envelope in Genevieve's hand, he walked on as rapidly as he could.

A few minutes later, standing under the light in the front hall, George Remington read this penciled note:

"I stood ready to contribute more than I promised—any amount to put you over. But if you give out a statement against suffrage you're a damn fool and I withdraw every cent. A man with no more political sense and skill than that isn't worth helping. You should have advised me.

"M. J."

II

BY HARRY LEON WILSON

It may have been surmised that our sterling young candidate for district attorney had not yet become skilled in dalliance with the equivocal; that he was no adept in ambiguity; that he would confront all issues with a rugged valiance susceptible of no misconstruction; that, in short, George Remington was no trimmer.

If he opposed an issue, one knew that he opposed it from the heart out. He said so and he meant it. And, being opposed to the dreadful heresy of equal suffrage, no reader of the Whitewater *Sentinel* that morning could say, as the shrewd so often say of our older statesmen, that George was "side-stepping."

Not George's the mellow gift, to say, in effect, that of course woman should vote the instant she wishes to, though perhaps that day has not yet come. Meantime the speaker boldly defies the world to show a man holding woman in loftier regard than he does, or ready to accord her a higher value in all true functions of the body politic. Equal suffrage, thank God, is inevitable at some future time, but until that glorious day when we can be assured that the sex has united in a demand for it, it were perhaps as well not to cloud the issues of the campaign now opening; though let it be understood, and he cannot put this too plainly, that he reveres the memory of his gray-haired mother without whose tender ministrations and wise guidance he could never have reached the height from which he now speaks. And so let us pass on to the voting on these canal bonds, the true inwardness of which, thanks to the venal activities of a corrupt opposition, even an exclusively male constituency has thus far failed to comprehend. And so forth.

Our hero, then, had yet to acquire this finesse. As we are now privileged to observe him, he is as easy to understand as the multiplication table, as little devious and, alas! as lacking in suavity.

Yet, let us be fair to George. Mere innocence of guile, of verbal trickery, had not alone sufficed for his passionate bluntness in the present crisis. At a later stage in his career as a husband he might have been equally blunt; yet never again, perhaps, would he have been so emotional in his opposition to woman polluting herself with the mire of politics.

Be it recalled that but five weeks had elapsed since George had solemnly promised to cherish and protect the fairest of the non-voting sex—at least in his State—and he was still taking his mission seriously. As he wrote the words that were now electrifying, in a manner of speaking, the readers of the *Sentinel,* and of neighboring journals with enough enterprise to secure them, he had beheld his own Genevieve, fine, flawless, tenderly nourished flower that she was, being dragged from her high place with the most distressing results.

He saw her rushed from the sacred shelter of her home and made to attend primaries; he saw her compelled to strive tearfully with problems that revolted all her finer instincts; he saw her insulted at polling booths; saw her voting in company with persons of both sexes whom one could never know.

He saw her tainted, bruised, beaten down in the struggle, losing little by little all sense of the holy values of Wife, Mother, Home. As he wrote he heard her weakening cries for help as she perished, and more than once his left arm instinctively curved to shield her.

Was it not for his wife, then; nay, for wifehood itself, that he wrote? And so, was it quite fair for unmarried Penfield Evans, burning at his breakfast table a cynical cigarette over the printed philippic, to murmur, "Gee! old George *has* spilled the beans!"

Simple words enough and not devoid of friendly concern. But should he not have divined that George had been appalled to his extremities of speech by the horrendous vision of his fair young bride being hurled into depths where she would be obliged, if not to have opinions of her own, at least to vote with the rabble as he might decide they ought to vote?

And should not other critics known to us have divined the racking anguish under which George had labored? For one, should

not Elizabeth Sheridan, amateur spinster, have been all sympathy
for one who was palpably more an alarmed bridegroom than a
mere candidate?

Should not her maiden heart have been touched by this plau-
sible aspect of George's dilemma, rather than her mere brain to
have been steeled to a humorous disparagement tinged with bitter-
ness?

And yet, "What rot!" muttered Miss Sheridan,—"silly rot, bally
rot, tommy rot, and all the other kinds!"

Hereupon she creased a brow not meant for creases and de-
faced an admirable nose with grievous wrinkles of disdain. "Sacred
names of wife and mother!" This seemed regrettably like swearing
as she delivered it, though she quoted verbatim. "Sacred names of
petted imbeciles!" she amended.

Then, with berserker fury, crumpling her *Sentinel* into a ball,
she venomously hurled it to the depths of a waste basket and reli-
giously rubbed the feel of it from her fingers. As she had not even
glanced at the column headed "Births, Deaths, Marriages," it will
be seen that her agitation was real.

And surely a more discerning sympathy might have been
looked for from the seasoned Martin Jaffry. A bachelor full of years
and therefore with illusions not only unimpaired but ripened, who
more quickly than he should have divined that his nephew for the
moment viewed all womankind as but one multiplied Genevieve,
upon whom it would be heinous to place the shackles of suffrage?

Perhaps Uncle Martin did divine this. Perhaps he was a mere
trimmer, a rank side-stepper, steeped in deceit and ever ready to
mouth the abominable phrase "political expediency." It were rash
to affirm this, for no analyst has ever fathomed the heart of a man
who has come to his late forties a bachelor by choice. One may but
guess from the ensuing meager data.

Uncle Martin at a certain corner of Maple Avenue that morning, fell in with Penfield Evans, who, clad as the lilies of a florist's
window, strode buoyantly toward his office, the vision of his day's
toil pinkly suffused by an overlaying vision of a Betty or Sheridan
character. Mr. Evans bubbled his greeting.

"Morning! Have you seen it? Oh, *say*, have you seen it?"

The immediate manner of Uncle Martin not less than his subdued garb of gray, his dark gloves and his somber stick, intimated that he saw nothing to bubble about.

"He has burned his bridges behind him." The speaker looked as grim as any bachelor-by-choice ever may.

"Regular little fire-bug," blithely responded Mr. Evans, moderating his stride to that of the other.

"Can't understand it," resumed the gloomy uncle. "I sent him word in time; sent it from your office by messenger. It was plain enough. I told him no money of mine would go into his campaign if he made a fool of himself—or words to that effect."

"Phew! Cast you off, did he? Just like that?"

"Just like that! Went out of his way to overdo it, too. Needn't have come out half so strong. No chance now to backwater—not a chance on earth to explain what he really did mean—and make it something different."

"Quixotic! That's how it reads to me."

Uncle Martin here became oracular, his somber stick gesturing to point his words.

"Trouble with poor George, he's been silly enough to blurt out the truth, what every man of us thinks in his heart—"

"Eh?" said Mr. Evans quickly, as one who has been jolted.

"No more sense than to come right out and say what every one of us thinks in his secret heart about women. I think it and you think it—"

"Oh, well, if you put it *that* way," admitted young Mr. Evans gracefully. "But of course—"

"Certainly, of *course!* We all think it—sacred names of home and mother and all the rest of it; but a man running for office these days is a chump to say so, isn't he? Of course he is! What chance does it leave him? Answer me that."

"Darned little, if you ask me," said Mr. Evans judicially. "Poor old George!"

"Talks as if he were going to be married tomorrow instead of its having come off five weeks ago," pursued Uncle Martin bitterly.

Plainly there were depths of understanding in the man, trimmer though he might be.

Mr. Evans made no reply. Irrationally he was considering the terms "five weeks" and "married" in relation to a spinster who would have professed to be indignant had she known it.

"Got to pull the poor devil out," said Uncle Martin, when in silence they had traversed fifty feet more of the shaded side of Maple Avenue.

"How?" demanded the again practical Mr. Evans.

"Make him take it back; make him recant; swing him over the last week before election. Make him eat his words with every sign of exquisite relish. Simple enough!"

"How?" persisted Mr. Evans.

"Wiles, tricks, subterfuges, chicanery—understand what I mean?"

"Sure! I understand what you mean as well as you do, but— come down to brass tacks."

"That's an entirely different matter," conceded Uncle Martin gruffly. "It may take thought."

"Oh, is that all? Very well then; we'll think. I, myself, will think. First, I'll have a talk with the sodden amorist. I'll grill him. I'll find the weak spot in his armor. There must be something we can put over on him."

"By fair means or foul," insisted Uncle Martin as they paused at the parting of their ways. "Lowdown, underhanded work—do you get what I mean?"

"I do, I do!" declared young Mr. Evans and broke once more into the buoyant stride of an earlier moment. This buoyance was interrupted but once, and briefly, ere he gained the haven of his office.

As he stepped quite too buoyantly into Fountain Square, he was all but run down by the new six-cylinder roadster of Mrs. Harvey Herrington, driven by the enthusiastic owner. He regained the curb in time, with a ready and heartfelt utterance nicely befitting the emergency.

The president of the Whitewater Women's Club, the Municipal League and the Suffrage Society, brought her toy to a stop fifteen feet beyond her too agile quarry, with a fine disregard for brakes and tire surfaces. She beckoned eagerly to him she might have slain. She was a large woman with an air of graceful but resolute authority; a woman good to look upon, attired with all deference to the modes of the moment, and exhaling an agreeable sense of good-will to all.

"Be careful always to look before you start across and you'll never have to say such things," was her greeting to Mr. Evans, as he halted beside this minor juggernaut.

"Sorry you heard it," lied the young man readily.

"Such a flexible little car—picks up before one realizes," conceded Whitewater's acknowledged social dictator. "But what I wanted to say is this: that poor daft partner of yours has mortally offended every woman in town except three, with that silly screed of his. I've seen nearly all of them that count this morning, or they've called me by telephone. Now, why couldn't he have had the advice of some good, capable woman before committing himself so rabidly?"

"Who were the three?" queried Mr. Evans.

"Oh, poor Genevieve, of course; she goes without saying. And you'd guess the other two if you knew them better—his cousin, Alys Brewster-Smith, and poor Genevieve's Cousin Emelene. They both have his horrible school-boy composition committed to memory, I do believe.

"Cousin Emelene recited most of it to me with tears in her weak eyes, and Alys tells me his noble words have made the world seem like a different place to her. She said she had been coming to believe that chivalry of the old true brand was dying out, but that dear Cousin George has renewed her faith in it.

"Think of poor Genevieve when they both fall on his neck. They're going up for that particular purpose this afternoon. The only two in town, mind you, except poor Genevieve. Oh, it's too awfully bad, because aside from this medieval view of his, George was probably as acceptable for this office as any man could be."

The lady burdened the word "man" with a tiny but distinguishable emphasis. Mr. Evans chose to ignore this.

"George's friends are going to take him in hand," said he. "Of course he was foolish to come out the way he has, even if he did say only what every man believes in his secret heart."

The president of the Whitewater Woman's Club fixed him with a glittering and suddenly hostile eye.

"What! you too?" she flung at him. He caught himself. He essayed explanations, modifications, a better lighting of the thing. But at the expiration of his first blundering sentence Mrs. Herrington, with her flexible little car, was narrowly missing an aged and careless pedestrian fifty yards down the street.

"George come in yet?"

For the second time Mr. Evans was demanding this of Miss Elizabeth Sheridan who had also ignored his preliminary "Good morning!"

Now for a moment more she typed viciously. One would have said that the thriving legal business of Remington and Evans required the very swift completion of the document upon which she wrought. And one would have been grossly deceived. The sheet had been drawn into the machine at the moment Mr. Evans' buoyant step had been heard in the outer hall, and upon it was merely written a dozen times the bald assertion, "Now is the time for all good men to come to the aid of the party."

Actually it was but the mechanical explosion of the performer's mood, rather than the wording of a sentiment now or at any happier time entertained by her.

At last she paused; she sullenly permitted herself to be interrupted. Her hands still hovered above the already well-punished keys of the typewriter. She glanced over a shoulder at Mr. Evans and allowed him to observe her annoyance at the interruption.

"George has not come in yet," she said coldly. "I don't think he will ever come in again. I don't see how he can have the face to. I shouldn't think he could ever show himself on the street again after that—that—"

The young woman's emotion overcame her at this point. Again her relentless fingers stung the blameless mechanism—"to come to the aid of the party. Now is the time for all good—" She here controlled herself to further speech. "And *you!* Of course you applaud him for it. Oh, I knew you were all alike!"

"Now look here, Betty, this thing has gone far enough—"

"Far enough, indeed!"

"But you won't give me a chance!"

Mr. Evans here bent above his employee in a threatening manner.

"You don't even ask what I think about it. You say I'm guilty and ought to be shot without a trial—not even waiting till sunrise. If you had the least bit of fairness in your heart you'd have asked me what I really thought about this outbreak of George's, and I'd have told you in so many words that I think he's made all kinds of a fool of himself."

"No! Do you really, Pen?"

Miss Sheridan had swiftly become human. She allowed her eyes to meet those of Mr. Evans' with an easy gladness but little known to him of late.

"Of course I do, Betty. The idea of a candidate for office in this enlightened age breaking loose in that manner! It's suicide. He could be arrested for the attempt in this State. Is that strong enough for you? You surely know how I feel now, don't you? Come on, Betty dear! Let's not spar in that foolish way any longer. Remember all I said yesterday. It goes double today—really, I see things more clearly."

Plainly Miss Sheridan was disarmed.

"And I thought you'd approve every word of his silly tirade," she murmured. Mr. Evans, still above her, was perilously shaken by the softer note in her voice, but he controlled himself in time and sat in one of the chairs reserved for waiting clients. It was near Miss Sheridan, yet beyond reaching distance. He felt that he must be cool in this moment of impending triumph.

"Wasn't it the awfullest rot?" demanded the spinster, pounding out a row of periods for emphasis.

"And he's got to be made to eat his words," said Mr. Evans, wisely taking the same by-path away from the one subject in all the world that really mattered.

"Who could make him?"

"I could, if I tried." It came in quiet, masterful tones that almost convinced the speaker himself.

"Oh, Pen, if you could! Wouldn't that be a victory, though? If you only could—"

"Well, if I only could—and if I do?" His intention was too pointed to be ignored.

"Oh, *that!*" He winced at the belittling "that." "Of course I couldn't promise—anyway I don't believe you could ever do it, so what's the use of being silly?"

"But you will—will you promise, if I *do* convert George? Answer the question, please!" Mr. Evans glared as only actual district attorneys have the right to.

"Oh, what nonsense—but, well, I'll promise—I'll promise to promise to think very seriously about it indeed, if you bring George around."

"Betty!" It was the voice of an able pleader and he half arose from his chair, his arms eloquent of purpose.

"'Now is the time for all good men to come to the aid of the party. Now is the time for'—" wrote Miss Sheridan with dazzling fingers, and the pleader resumed his seat.

"How will you bring him 'round," she then demanded.

"Wiles, tricks, stratagems," replied the rising young diplomat moodily, smarting under the moment's defeat.

"Serve him right for pulling all that old-fashioned nonsense," said Miss Sheridan, and accorded her employer a glance in which admiration for his prowess was not half concealed.

"The words of a fool wise in his own folly," went on the encouraged Mr. Evans, and then, alas! a victim to the slight oratorical thrill these words brought him,—"honestly uttering what every last man believes and feels about woman in his heart and yet what no sane man running for office can say in public—here, what's the matter?"

The latter clause had been evoked by the sight of a blazing Miss Sheridan, who now stood over him with fists tightly clenched.

"Oh, oh, oh!" This was low, tense, thrilling. It expressed horror. "So that's what your convictions amount to! Then you do applaud him, every word of him, and you were deceiving me. Every man in his own heart, indeed. Thank heaven I found you out in time!"

It may be said that Mr. Evans now cowered in his chair. The term is not too violent. He ventured to lift a hand in weak protest.

"No, no, Betty, you are being unjust to me again. I meant that that was what Martin Jaffry told me this morning. It isn't what I believe at all. I tell you my own deepest sentiments are exactly what yours are in this great cause which—which—"

Painfully he became aware of his own futility. Miss Sheridan had ceased to blaze. Seated again before the typewriter she grinned at him with amused incredulity.

"You nearly had me going, Pen."

Mr. Evans summoned the deeper resources of his manhood and achieved an easier manner. He brazenly returned her grin.

"I'll have you going again before I'm through—remember that."

"By wiles, tricks and stratagems, I suppose."

"The same. By those I shall make poor George recant, and by those, assuming you to be a woman with a fine sense of honor who will hold a promise sacred, I shall have you going. And, mark my words, you'll be going good, too!

"Silly!"

She drew from the waste basket the maltreated *Sentinel,* unfurled it to expose the offending matter, and smote the column with the backs of four accusing fingers.

"There, my dear, is your answer. Now run along like a good boy."

"Silly!" said Mr. Evans, striving for a masterly finish to the unequal combat. He arose, dissembling cheerful confidence, straightened the frame of a steel-engraved Daniel Webster on the wall, and thrice paced the length of the room, falsely appearing to be engaged in deep thought.

Miss Sheridan, apparently for mere exclamatory purposes, now reread the fulmination of the absent partner. She scoffed, she sneered, flouted, derided, and one understood that she was including both members of the firm. Then her listener became aware that she had achieved coherence.

"Indeed, yes! Do you know what ought to happen to him? Every unprotected female in this county ought to pack her trunk and trudge right up to the Remington place and say, 'Here we are, noble man! We have read your burning words in which you offer to protect us. Save us from the vote! Let your home be our sanctuary. That's what you mean if you meant anything but tommy-rot.

Here and now we throw ourselves upon your boasted chivalry. Where are our rooms, and what time is luncheon served.'"

"Here! Just say that again," called Mr. Evans from across the room. Miss Sheridan obliged. She elaborated her theme. George should be taken at his word by every weak flower of womanhood. If women were nothing but ministering angels, it was "up to" George to give 'em a chance to minister.

So went Miss Sheridan's improvisation and Mr. Evans, suffering the throes of a mighty inspiration, suddenly found it sweetest music.

When Miss Sheridan subsided, Mr. Evans appeared to have forgotten the cause of their late encounter. Whistling cheerily he bustled into his own office, mumbling of matters that had to be "gotten off." For some moments he busied himself at his desk, then emerged to dictate three business letters to his late antagonist.

He dictated in a formal and distant manner, pausing in the midst of the last letter to spell out the word "analysis," which he must have known would enrage her further. Then, quite casually, he wished to be told if she might know the local habitat of Mrs. Alys Brewster-Smith and a certain Cousin Emelene. His manner was arid.

Miss Sheridan chanced to know that the ladies were sheltered in the exclusive boarding-house of one Mrs. Gallup, out on Erie Street, and informed him to this effect in the fewest possible words. Mr. Evans whistled absently a moment, then formally announced that he should be absent from the office for perhaps an hour.

Hat, gloves and stick in hand, he was about to nod punctiliously to the back of Miss Sheridan's head when the door opened to admit none other than our hero, George Remington. George wore the look of one who is uplifted and who yet has found occasion to be thoughtful about it. Penfield Evans grasped his hand and shook it warmly.

"Fine, George, old boy—simply corking! Honestly, I didn't believe you had it in you. You covered the ground and you did it in a big way. It took nerve, all right! Of course you probably know that every woman in town is speaking of your young wife as 'poor Genevieve,' but you've had the courage of your convictions. It's great!"

"Thanks, old man! I've spoken for the right as I saw it, let come what may. By the way, has Uncle Martin been in this morning, or telephoned, or sent any word?"

Miss Sheridan coldly, signified that none of these things had occurred, whereupon George sighed in an interesting manner and entered his own room.

Mr. Evans had uttered his congratulations in clear, ringing tones and Miss Sheridan, even as she wrote, contrived with her trained shoulders to exhibit to his lingering eye an overwhelming contempt for his opinions and his double-dealing.

In spite of which he went out whistling, and closed the door in a defiant manner.

III

BY FANNIE HURST

DESTINY, busybody that she is, has her thousand irons in her perpetual fires, turning, testing and wielding them.

While Miss Betty Sheridan, for another scornful time, was rereading the well-thumbed copy of the *Sentinel,* her fine back arched like a prize cat's, George Remington in his small mahogany office adjoining, neck low and heels high, was codifying, over and over again, the small planks of his platform, stuffing the knot holes which afforded peeps to the opposite side of the issue with anti-putty, and planning a bombardment of his pattest phrases for the complete capitulation of his Uncle Jaffry.

While Genevieve Remington in her snug library, so eager in her wifeliness to clamber up to her husband's small planks, and if need be, spread her prettily flounced skirts over the rotting places, was, memorizing, with more pride than understanding, extracts from the controversial article for quotation at the Woman's Club meeting, Mr. Penfield Evans, with a determination which considerably expanded his considerable chest measurement, ran two at a bound up the white stone steps of Mrs. Gallup's private boarding-house and pulled out the white china knob of a bell that gave no evidence of having sounded within, and left him uncertain to ring again.

A cast-iron deer, with lichen growing along its antlers, stood poised for instant flight in Mrs. Gallup's front yard.

While Mr. Evans waited he regarded its cast-iron flanks, but not seeingly. His rather the expression of one who stares into the future and smiles at what he sees.

Erie Street, shaded by a double row of showy chestnuts, lay in summer calm. A garden hose with a patent attachment spun spray over an adjoining lawn and sent up a greeny smell. Out from under the striped awning of Hassebrock's Ice Cream Parlor, cat-a-corner,

Percival Pauncefort Sheridan, in rubber-heeled canvas shoes and white trousers, cuffed high, emerged and turned down Huron Street, making frequent forays into a bulging rear pocket.

Miss Lydia Chipley, vice-president of the Busy Bee Sewing and Civic Club, cool, starchy and unhatted, clicked past on slim, trim heels, all radiated by the reflection from a pink parasol, gay embroidery bag dangling.

"Hello, Lyd!"

"Hello, Pen!"

"What's your hurry?"

"It's my middle name."

"Why hurry, when the future is always waiting?"

"Why aren't you holding your partner's head since he committed political suicide in the *Sentinel?*"

"I'd rather hold your head, Lyd, any day in the week."

"Gaul," said Miss Chipley, passing on, her sharply etched little face glowing in the pink reflection of the parasol, "is bounded on the north by Mrs. Gallup's boarding-house, and on the south by—"

"By the Frigid Zone!"

Then the door from behind swung open. Mr. Penfield Evans stepped into Mrs. Gallup's cool, exclusive parlor of better days, and delivering his card to a moist-fingered maid, sat himself among the shrouded furniture to await Mrs. Alys Brewster-Smith and Miss Emelene Brand.

Mrs. Gallup's boarding-house was finishing its noonday meal. Boiled odors lay upon a parlor that was otherwise redolent of the more opulent days of the Gallups. A not too ostentatious clatter of dishes came through the closed folding-doors.

Almost immediately Mrs. Alys Brewster-Smith, her favorite Concentrated Breath of the Lily always in advance, rustled into the darkened parlor, her stride hitting vigorously into her black taffeta skirts. Even as she shook hands with Mr. Evans, she jerked the window shade to its height, so that her smoothness and coloring shone out above her weeds.

In the shadow of her and at her life job of bringing up the rear, with a large Maltese cat padding beside her, entered Miss Brand on rubber heels. She was the color of long twilight.

Mr. Evans rose to his six-feet-in-his-stockings and extended them each a hand, Miss Emelene drawing the left.

Mrs. Smith threw up a dainty gesture, black lace ruffles falling back from arms all the whiter because of them.

"Well, Penny Evans!"

"None other, Mrs. Smith, than the villain himself."

"Be seated, Penfield."

"Thanks, Miss Emelene."

They drew up in a triangle beside the window overlooking the cast-iron deer. The cat sprang up, curling in the crotch of Miss Emelene's arm.

"Nice ittie kittie, say how-do to big Penny-field-Evans. Say how-do to big man. Say how-do, muvver's ittie kittie." Miss Emelene extended the somewhat reluctant Maltese paw, five hook-shaped claws slightly in evidence.

"Say how-do to Hanna, Penfield. Hanna, say how-do to big man."

"How-do, Hanna," said Mr. Evans, reddening slightly beneath his tan. Then hitched his chair closer.

"To what," he began, flashing his white smile from one to the other of them, and with a strong veer to the facetious, "are we indebted for the honor of this visit? Are those the unspoken words, ladies?"

"Nothing wrong at home, Penfield? Nobody ailing or—"

"No, no, Miss Emelene, never better. As a matter of fact, it's a piece of political business that has prompted me to—"

At that Mrs. Smith jangled her bracelets, leaning forward on her knees.

"If it's got anything to do with your partner and my cousin George Remington having the courage to go in for the district attorneyship without the support of the vote-hunting, vote-eating women of this town, I'm here to tell you that I'm with him heart and soul. He can have my support and—"

"Mine too. And if I've got anything to say my two nephews will vote for him; and I think I have, with my two heirs."

"Ladies, it fills my heart with joy to—"

"Votes! Why what would the powder-puffing, short-skirted,

bridge-playing women of this town do with the vote if they had it?
Wear it around their necks on a gold chain?"

"Well spoken, Mrs. Smith, if—"

"I know the direction you lean, Penfield Evans, letting—"

"But, Miss Emelene, I—"

"Letting that shameless Betty Sheridan, a girl that had as sweet
and womanly a mother as Whitewater ever boasted, lead you
around by the nose on her suffrage string. A girl with her raising
and both of her grandmothers women that lived and died genteel,
to go traipsing around in her low heels in men's offices and ad-
dressing hoi polloi from soap boxes! Why, between her and that female chauffeur, Mrs. Herrington, another woman whose mother
was of too fine feelings even to join the Delsarte class, the women
of this town are being influenced to making disgraceful—dis—oh,
what shall I say, Alys?"

Here Mrs. Smith broke in, thumping a soft fist into a soft palm.

"It's the most pernicious movement, Mr. Evans, that has ever
got hold of this community and we need a man like my cousin
George Remington to—"

"But, Mrs. Smith, that's just what I—"

"To stamp it out! Stamp it out! It's eating into the homes of
Whitewater, trying to make breadwinners out of the creatures God
intended for the bread-eaters—I mean bread-bakers."

"But, Mrs. Smith, I—"

"Woman's place has been the home since home was a cave, and
it will be the home so long as women will remember that womanliness is their greatest asset. As poor dear Mr. Smith was so fond of
saying, he—I can't bring myself to talk of him, Mr. Evans, but—but
as he used to say, I—"

"Yes, yes, Mrs. Smith, I understa—"

"But as my cousin says in his article, which in my mind should
be spread broadcast, what higher mission for woman than—than—
just what are his words, Emelene?"

Miss Brand leaned forward, her gaze boring into space.

"What higher mission," she quoted, as if talking in a chapel,
"for woman than that she sit enthroned in the home, wielding her
invisible but mighty scepter from that throne, while man, kissing

the hand that so lovingly commands him, shall bear her gifts and do her bidding. That is the strongest vote in the world. That is the universal suffrage which chivalry grants to woman. The unpolled vote! Long may it reign!"

Round spots of color had come out on Miss Emelene's long cheeks.

"A man who can think like that has the true—the true—what shall I say, Alys?"

"But, ladies, I protest that I'm not—"

"Has the true chivalry of spirit, Emelene, that the women are too stark raving mad to appreciate. You can't come here, Mr. Evans, to two women to whom womanliness and love of home, thank God, are still uppermost and try to convert us to—"

Here Mr. Evans executed a triple gyration, to the annoyance of Hanna, who withdrew from the gesture, and raised his voice to a shout that was not without a note of command.

"Convert you! Why women alive, what I've been bursting a blood vessel trying to say during the length of this interview is that I'd as soon dip my soul in boiling oil as try to convert you away from the cause. *My* cause! *Our* cause!"

"Why—"

"I'm here to tell you that I'm with my partner head-over-heels on the plank he has taken."

"But we thought—"

"We thought you and Betty Sheridan—why, my cousin Genevieve Remington told me that—"

"Yes, yes, Miss Emelene. But not even the wiles of a pretty woman can hold out indefinitely against Truth! A broad-minded man has got to keep the door of his mind open to conviction, or it decays of mildew. I confess that finally I am convinced that if there is one platform more than another upon which George Reming-ton deserves his election it is on the brave and chivalrous principles he has so courageously come out with in the current *Sentinel*. Whatever may have been between Betty Sheridan and—"

"Mr. Evans, you don't mean to tell me that you and Betty Sheridan have quarreled! Such a desirable match from every point of view, family and all! It goes to show what a rattle-pated bunch of women they are! Any really clever girl with an eye to her future, anti or pro, could shift her politics when it came to a question of matri—"

"Mrs. Smith, there comes a time in every modern man's life when he's got to keep his politics and his pretty girls separate, or suffrage will get him if he don't watch out!"

"Yes, and Mr. Evans, if what I hear is true, a good-looking woman can talk you out of your safety deposit key!"

"That's where you're wrong, Mrs. Smith, and I'll prove it to you. Despite any wavering I may have exhibited, I now stand, as George puts it in his article, 'ready to conserve the threatened flower of womanhood by also endeavoring to conserve her un-polled vote!' If you women want prohibition, it is in your power to sway man's vote to prohibition. If you women want the moon, let man cast your proxy vote for it! In my mind, that is the true chivalry. To quote again, 'Woman is man's rarest heritage, his beautiful responsibility, and at all times his co-operation, support and protection are due her. His support and protection.'"

Miss Emelene closed her eyes. The red had spread in her cheeks and she laid her head back against the chair, rocking softly and stroking the thick-napped cat.

"The flower of womanhood," she repeated. "'His support and his protection.' If ever a man deserved high office because of high principles, it's my cousin George Remington! My cousin Genevieve Livingston Remington is the luckiest girl in the world, and not one of us Brands but what is willing to admit it. My two nephews, too, if their Aunt Emelene has anything to say, and I think she has—"

"Why, there isn't a stone in the world I wouldn't turn to see that boy in office," Mrs. Smith interrupted.

At that Mr. Evans rose.

"You mean that, Mrs. Smith?"

Miss Emelene rose with him, the cat pouring from her lap.

"Of course she means it, Penfield. What self-respecting woman wouldn't!"

Mr. Evans sat down again suddenly, Miss Emelene with him, and leaning violently forward, thrust his eager, sun-tanned face between the two women.

"Well, then, ladies, here's your chance to prove it! That's what brings me today. As two of the self-respecting, idealistic and womanly women of this community, I have come to urge you both to—"

"Oh, Mr. Evans!"

"Penfield, you are the flatterer!"

"To induce two such representative women as yourselves to help my partner to the election he so well deserves."

"Us?"

"It is in your power, ladies, to demonstrate to Whitewater that George Remington's chivalry is not only on paper, but in his soul."

"But—how?"

"By throwing yourselves upon his generosity and hospitality, at least during the campaign. You have it in your power, ladies, to strengthen the only uncertain plank upon which George Remington stands today."

A clock ticked roundly into a silence tinged with eloquence. The Maltese leaped back into Miss Emelene's lap, purring there.

"You mean, Penfield, for us to go visit George—er—er—"

"Just that! Bag and baggage. As two relatives and two unattached women, it is your privilege, nay, your right."

"But—"

"He hasn't come out in words with it, but he has intimated that such an act from the representative antis of this town would more than anything strengthen his theories into facts. As unattached women, particularly as women of his own family, his support and protection, as he puts it, are due you, *due* you!"

Mrs. Smith clasped her plentifully ringed fingers, and regarded him with her prominent eyes widening.

"Why, I—unprotected widow that I am, Mr. Evans, am not the one to force myself even upon my cousin if—"

"Nor I, Penfield. It would be a pleasant enough change, heaven knows, from the boarding-house. But you can ask your mother, Penfield, if there ever was a prouder girl in all Whitewater than Emmy Brand. I—"

"But, I tell you, ladies, the obligation is all on George's part. It's just as if you were polling votes for him. What is probably the oldest adage in the language, states that actions speak louder than words. Give him his chance to spread broadcast to your sex his protection, his support. That, ladies, is all I—we—ask."

"But I—Genevieve—the housekeeping, Penfield. Genevieve isn't much on management when it comes to—"

"Housekeeping! Why, I have it from your fair cousin herself, Miss Emelene, that her idea of their new little home is the Open House."

"Yes, but—as Emelene says, Mr. Evans, it's an imposition to—"

"Why do you think, Mrs. Smith, Martin Jaffry spends all his evenings up at Remingtons' since they're back from their honeymoon? Why, he was telling me only last night it's for the joy of seeing that new little niece of his lording it over her well-oiled little household, where a few extra dropping in makes not one whit of difference."

At this remark, embedded like a diamond in a rock, a shade of faintest color swam across Mrs. Smith's face and she swung him her profile and twirled at her rings.

"And where Genevieve Remington's husband's interests are involved, ladies, need I go further in emphasizing your welcome into that little home?"

"Heaven knows it would be a change from the boarding-house, Alys. The lunches here are beginning to go right against me! That sago pudding today—and Gallup knowing how I hate starchy desserts!"

"For the sake of the cause, Miss Emelene, too!"

"Gallup would have to hold our rooms at half rate."

"Of course, Mrs. Smith. I'll arrange all that."

"I—I can't go over until evening, with three trunks to pack."

"Just fine, Mrs. Smith. You'll be there just in time to greet George at dinner."

Miss Emelene fell to stroking the cat, again curled like a sardelle in her lap.

"Kitti-kitti-kitti—, does muvver's ittsie Hanna want to go on visit to Tousin George in fine new ittie house? To fine Tousin Georgie what give ittsie Hanna big saucer milk evvy day? Big fine George what like ladies and lady kitties!"

"Emelene, it's out of the question to take Hanna. You know how George Remington hates cats! You remember at the Sunday School Bazaar when—"

A grimness descended like a mask over Miss Brand's features. Her mouth thinned.

"Very well, then. Without Hanna you can count me out, Penfield. If—"

"No, no! Why nonsense, Miss Emelene! George doesn't—"

"This cat has the feelings and sensibilities of a human being."

"Why of course," cried Penfield Evans, reaching for his hat. "Just you bring Hanna right along, Miss Emelene. That's only a pet pose of George's when he wants to tease his relatives, Mrs. Smith. I remember from college—why I've seen George *kiss* a cat!"

Miss Emelene huddled the object of controversy up in her chin, talking down into the warm gray fur.

"Was 'em tryin' to 'buse muvver's ittsie bittsie kittsie? Muvver's ittsie bittsie kittsie!"

They were in the front hall now, Mr. Evans tugging at the door.

"I'll run around now and arrange to have your trunks called for at five. My congratulations and thanks, ladies, for helping the right man toward the right cause."

"You're *sure*, Penfield, we'll be welcome?"

"Welcome as the sun that shines!"

"If I thought, Penfield, that Hanna wouldn't be welcome I wouldn't budge a step."

"Of course she's welcome, Miss Emelene. Isn't she of the gentler sex? There'll be a cab around for you and Mrs. Smith and Hanna about five. So long, Mrs. Smith, and many thanks. Miss Emelene, Hanna."

On the outer steps they stood for a moment in a dapple of sunshine and shadow from chestnut trees.

"Good-by, Mr. Evans, until evening."

"Good-by, Mrs. Smith." He paused on the walk, lifting his hat and flashing his smile a third time.

"Good-by, Miss Emelene."

From the steps Miss Brand executed a rotary motion with the left paw of the dangling Maltese.

"Tell nice gentleman by-by. Tum now, Hanna, get washed and new ribbon to go by-by. Her go to big Cousin George and piddy Cousin Genevieve. By-by! By-by!" The door swung shut, enclosing them. Down the quiet, tree-shaped sidewalk, Mr. Penfield Evans strode into the somnolent afternoon, turning down Huron Street. At the remote end of the block and before her large frame mansion of a thousand angles and wooden lace work, Mrs. Harvey Herrington's low car sidled to her curb-stone, racy-looking as a hound. That lady herself, large and modish, was in the act of stepping up and in.

"Well, Pen Evans! 'Tis writ in the book our paths should cross."

"Who more pleased than I?"

"Which way are you bound?"

"Jenkins' Transfer and Cab Service."

"Jump in."

"No sooner said than done."

Mrs. Herrington threw her clutch and let out a cough of steam. They jerked and leaped forward. From the rear of the car an orange and black pennant—*Votes for Women*—stiffened out like a semaphore against the breeze.

IV

BY DOROTHY CANFIELD

GENEVIEVE REMINGTON sat in her pretty drawing-room and watched the hour hand of the clock slowly approach five. Five was a sacred hour in her day. At five George left his office, turned off the business-current with a click and turned on, full-voltage, the domestic-affectionate.

Genevieve often told her girl friends that she only began really to live after five, when George was restored to her. She assured them the psychical connection between George and herself was so close that, sitting alone in her drawing-room, she could feel a tingling thrill all over when the clock struck five and George emerged from his office downtown.

On the afternoon in question she received her five o'clock electric thrill promptly on time, although history does not record whether or not George walked out from his office at that moment. With all due respect for the world-shaking importance of Mr. Remington's movements, it must be stated that history had, on that afternoon, other more important events to chronicle.

As the clock struck five, the front doorbell rang. Marie, the maid, went to open the door. Genevieve adjusted the down-sweeping, golden-brown tress over her right eye, brushed an invisible speck from the piano, straightened a rose in a vase, and after these traditionally bridal preparations, waited with a bride's optimistic smile the advent of a caller. But it was Marie who appeared at the door, with a stricken face of horror.

"Mrs. Remington! Mrs. Remington!" she whispered loudly. "They've come to stay. The men are getting their trunks down from the wagon."

"*Who* has come to stay? *Where?*" queried the startled bride.

"The two ladies who came to call yesterday!"

"Oh!" said the relieved Genevieve. "There's some mistake, of course. If it's Cousin Emelene and Mrs.—"

She advanced into the hall and was confronted by two burly men with a very large trunk between them.

"Which room?" said one of them in a bored and insolent voice.

"Oh, you must have come to the wrong house," Genevieve assured them with her pretty, friendly smile.

She was so happy and so convinced of the essential rightness of a world which had produced George Remington that she had a friendly smile for every one, even for unshaven men who kept their battered derby hats on their heads, bad viciously smelling cigars in their mouths, and penetrated to her sacred front hall with trunks which belonged somewhere else.

"Isn't this G. L. Remington's house?" inquired one of the men, dropping his end of the trunk and consulting a dirty slip of paper.

"Yes, it is," admitted Genevieve, thrilling at the thought that it was also hers.

"This is the place all right, then," said the man. He heaved up his end of the trunk again, and said once more, "Which room?"

The repetition fell a little ominously on Genevieve's ear. What on earth could be the matter? She heard voices outside and craning her soft white neck, she saw Cousin Emelene, with her gray kitten under one arm and a large suitcase in her other hand, coming up the steps. There was a beatific expression in her gentle, faded eyes, and her lips were quivering uncertainly. When she caught sight of Genevieve's sweet face back of the bored expressman, she gave a little cry, ran forward, set down her suitcase and clasped her young cousin in her arms.

"Oh Genevieve dear, that noble wonderful husband of yours! What have you done to deserve such a man . . . out of this Age of Gold!"

This was a sentiment after Genevieve's own heart, but she found it rather too vague to meet the present somewhat tense situation.

Cousin Emelene went on, clasping her at intervals, and talking very fast.

"I can hardly believe it! Now that my time of trial is all over I don't mind telling you that I was growing embittered and cynical. All those phrases my dear mother had brought me to believe, the sanctity of the home, the chivalrous protection of men, the wicked folly of women who leave the home to engage in fierce industrial struggle." . . . At about this point the expressman set the trunk down, put their hands on their hips, cocked their hats at a new angle and waited in gloomy ennui for the conversation to stop. Cousin Emelene flowed on, her voice unsteady with a very real emotion.

"See, dear, you must not blame me for my lack of faith . . . but see how it looked to me. There I was, as womanly a woman as ever breathed, and yet *I* had no home to be sanctified, *I* had never had a bit of chivalrous protection from any man. And with the New Haven stocks shrinking from one day to the next, the way they do, it looked as though I would either have to starve or engage in the wicked, unwomanly folly of earning my own living.

"Do you know, dear Genevieve, I had almost come to the point—you know how the suffragists do keep banging away at their points—I almost wondered if perhaps they were right and if men really *mean* those things about protection and support in place of the vote. . . . And then George's splendid, noble-spirited article appeared, and a kind friend interpreted it for me and told what it really meant, for *me!* Oh, Genevieve." . . . The tears rose to her mild eyes, her gentle, flat voice faltered, she took out a handkerchief hastily. "It seemed too good to be true," she said brokenly into its folds. "I've longed all my life to be protected, and now I'm going to be!"

"Which room, please?" said the expressman. "We gotta be goin' on."

Genevieve pinched herself hard, jumped and said *"ouch."* Yes, she was awake, all right!

"Oh, Marie, will you please get Hanna a saucer of milk?" said Cousin Emelene now, seeing the maid's round eyes glaring startled from the dining-room door. "And just warm it a little bit, don't scald it. She won't touch it if there's the least bit of a scum on it. Just take that ice-box chill off. Here, I'll go with you this time.

Since we're going to live here now, you'll have to do it a good many times, and I'd better show you just how to do it right."

She disappeared, leaving a trail of caressing baby-talk to the effect that she would take good care of muvver's ittie bittie kittie. She left Genevieve for all practical purposes turned to stone. She felt as though she were stone, from head to foot, and she could open her mouth no more than any statue when, in answer to the next repetition, very peremptory now, of "Which room?" a voice as peremptory called from the open front door, "Straight upstairs; turn to your right, first door on the left."

As the men started forward, banging the mahogany banisters with the corners of the trunk at every step, Mrs. Brewster-Smith stepped in, immaculate as to sheer collar and cuffs, crisp and tailored as to suit, waved and netted as to hair, and chilled steel and diamond point as to will-power.

"Oh, Genevieve, I didn't see *you* there! I didn't know why they stood there waiting so long. I know the house so well I knew of course which room you'll have for guests. *Dear* old house! It will be like returning to my childhood to live here again!" She cocked an ear toward the upper regions and frowned, but went on smoothly.

"Such happy girlhood hours as I have passed here! After all there is nothing like the home feeling, is there, for us women at any rate! We're the natural conservatives, who cling to the simple, elemental satisfactions, and there's a heart-hunger that can only be satisfied by a home and a man's protection! I thought George's description too beautiful . . . in his article you know . . . of the ideal home with the women of the family safe within its walls, protected from the savagery of the economic struggle which only men in their strength can bear without being crushed."

She turned quickly and terribly to the expressmen coming down the stairs and said in so fierce a voice that they shrank back visibly, "There's another trunk to take up to the room next to that. And if you let it down with the bang you did this one, you'll get something that will surprise you! Do you hear me!"

They shrank out, cowed and tiptoeing. Mrs. Brewster-Smith turned back to her young cousin-by-marriage and murmured,

"That was such a true and deep saying of George's . . . wherever does such a young man get his wisdom! . . . that women are not fitted by nature to cope with hostile forces!"

Cousin Emelene approached from behind the statue of Genevieve, still frozen in place with an expression of stupefaction on her white face. The older woman put her arms around the bride's neck and gave her an affectionate hug.

"Oh, dearest Jinny, doesn't it seem like a dream that we're all going to be together, all we women, in a real home, with a real man at the head of it to direct us and give us of his strength! It does seem just like that beautiful old-fashioned home that George drew such an exquisite picture of, in his article, where the home was the center of the world to the women in it. It will be to me, I assure you, dear. I feel as though I had come to a haven, and as though I *never* would want to leave it!"

The expressmen were carrying up another trunk now, and so conscious of the glittering eyes of mastery upon them that they carried it as though it were the Ark of the Covenant and they its chosen priests. Mrs. Brewster-Smith followed them with a firm tread, throwing over her shoulder to the stone Genevieve below, "Oh, my dear, little Eleanor and her nurse will be in soon. Frieda was taking Eleanor for her usual afternoon walk. Will you just send them upstairs when they come! I suppose Frieda will have the room in the third story, that extra room that was finished off when Uncle Henry lived here. Emelene, you'd better come right up, too, if you expect to get unpacked before dinner."

She disappeared, and Emelene fluttered up after her, drawn along by suction, apparently, like a sheet of paper in the wake of a train. The expressmen came downstairs, still treading softly, and went out. Genevieve was alone again in her front hall.

To her came tiptoeing Marie, with wide eyes of query and alarm. And from Marie's questioning face, Genevieve fled away like one fleeing from the plague.

"Don't ask me, Marie! Don't *speak* to me. Don't you dare ask me what . . . or I'll . . ." She was at the front door as she spoke, poised for flight like a terrified doe. "I must see Mr. Remington! I don't know *what* to tell you, Marie, till I have seen Mr. Remington!

I must see my husband! I don't know what to say, I don't know what to *think*, until I have seen my husband."

Calling this eminently wifely sentiment over her shoulder she ran down the front walk, hatless, wrapless, just as she was in her pretty flowered and looped-up bride's house dress. She couldn't have run faster if the house had been on fire.

The clicking of her high heels on the concrete sidewalk was a rattling tattoo so eloquent of disorganized panic that more than one head was thrust from a neighboring window to investigate, and more than one head was pulled back, nodding to the well-worn and charitable hypothesis, "Their first quarrel." The hypothesis would instantly have been withdrawn if any one had continued looking after the fleeing bride long enough to see her, regardless of passers-by, fling herself wildly into her husband's arms as he descended from the trolleycar at the corner.

Betty Sheridan was sitting in the drawing-room of her parents' house, rather moodily reading a book on the *Balance of Trade.*

She had an unconfessed weakness of mind on the subject of tariffs and international trade. Although when in college she had written a paper on it which had been read aloud in the Economics Seminar and favorably commented upon, she knew, in her heart of hearts, that she understood less than nothing about the underlying principles of the subject. This nettled her and gave her occasional nightmare moments of doubt as to the real fitness of women for public affairs. She read feverishly all she could find on the subject, ending by addling her brains to the point of frenzy.

She was almost in that condition now although she did not look it in the least as, dressed for dinner in the evening gown which replaced the stark linens and tailored seams of her office-costume, she bent her shining head and earnest face over the pages of the book.

Penfield Evans took a long look at her, as one looks at a rose-bush in bloom, before he spoke through the open door and broke the spell.

"Oh, Betty," he called in a low tone, beckoning her with a gesture redolent of mystery.

Betty laid down her book and stared. "What you want?" she

challenged him, reverting to the phrase she had used when they were children together.

"Come on out here a minute!" he said, jerking his head over his shoulder. "I want to show you something."

"Oh, I can't fuss around with you," said Betty, turning to her book again. "I've got Roberts' *Balance of Trade* out of the library and I must finish it by tomorrow." She began to read again.

The young man stood silent for a moment.

"Great Scott!" he was saying to himself with a sinking heart. "*So that's* what they pick up for light reading, when they're waiting for dinner!"

He had a particularly gone feeling because, although he had made several successful political speeches on international trade and foreign tariffs, he was intelligent enough to know in his heart of hearts that he had no real understanding of the principles involved. He had come, indeed, to doubt if any one had!

Now, as he watched the pretty sleek head bent over the book he had supposed of course was a novel, he felt a qualm of real apprehension. Maybe there was something in what that guy said, the one who wrote a book to prove (bringing Queen Elizabeth and Catherine the Great as examples) that the real genius of women is for political life. Maybe they *have* a special gift for it! Maybe, a generation or so from now, it'll be the *men* who are disfranchised for incompetence. . . . He put away as fantastic such horrifying ideas, and with a quick action of his resolute will applied himself to the present situation.

"Oh Betty, you don't know what you're missing! It's a sight you'll never forget as long as you live . . . oh, come on! Be a sport. Take a chance!"

Betty was still suspicious of frivolity, but she rose, looked at her wrist-watch and guessed she'd have a few minutes before dinner, to fool away in light-minded society.

"There's nothing light-minded about this!" Penny assured her gravely, leading her swiftly down the street, around the corner, up another street and finally, motioning her to silence, up on the well-clipped lawn of a handsome, dignified residence, set around with old trees.

"Look!" he whispered in her ear, dramatically pointing in through the lighted window. "Look! What do you see?"

Betty looked, and looked again and turned on him petulantly: "What foolishness are you up to now, Penfield Evans!" she whispered energetically. "Why under the sun did you drag me out to see Emelene and Alys Brewster-Smith dining with the Remingtons? Isn't it just the combination of reactionary old fogies you might expect to get together . . . though I didn't know Alys ever took her little girl out to dinner-parties, and Emelene must be perfectly crazy over that cat to take her here. Cats make George's flesh creep. Don't you remember, at the Sunday School Bazaar."

He cut her short with a gesture of command, and applying his lips to her ear so that he would not be heard inside the house, he said, "You think all you see is Emelene and Alys taking dinner *en famille* with the Remingtons. Eyes that see not! What you are gazing upon is a reconstruction of the blessed family life that existed in the good old days, before the industrial period and the abominable practice of economic independence for women began! You are seeing Woman in her proper place, the Home, . . . if not her own Home, somebody's Home, anybody's Home . . . the Home of the man nearest to her, who owes her protection because she can't vote. You are gazing upon . . ."

His rounded periods were silenced by a tight clutch on his wrist.

"Penfield Evans. Don't you dare exaggerate to me! Have they come there to stay! *To take him at his word!*"

He nodded solemnly.

"Their trunks are upstairs in the only two spare-rooms in the house, and Frieda is installed in the only extra room in the attic. Marie gave notice that she was going to quit, just before dinner. George has been telephoning to my Aunt Harriet to see if she knows of another maid. . . ."

"Whatever . . . whatever could have made them *think* of such a thing!" gasped Betty, almost beyond words.

"I did!" said Penfield Evans, tapping himself on the chest. "It was *my* giant intelligence that propelled them here."

He was conscious of a lacy rush upon him, and of a couple of soft arms which gave him an impassioned embrace none the less vigorous because the arms were more used to tennis-racquets and canoe-paddles than impassioned embraces. Then he was thrust back . . . and there was Betty, collapsed against a lilac bush, shaking and convulsed, one hand pressed hard on her mouth to keep back the shrieks of merriment which continually escaped in suppressed squeals, the other hand outstretched toward him off. . . .

"No, don't you touch me, I didn't mean a thing by it! I just couldn't help it! It's too, *too* rich! Oh Penny, you duck! Oh, I shall die! I shall die! I never saw anything so funny in my life! Oh, Penny, take me away or I shall perish here and now!"

On the whole, in spite of the repulsing hand, he took it that he had advanced his cause. He broke into a laugh, more light-hearted than he had uttered for a long time. They stood for a moment more in the soft darkness, gazing in with rapt eyes at the family scene. Then they reeled away up the street, gasping and choking with mirth, festooning themselves about trees for support when their legs gave way under them.

"*Did* you see George's face when Emelene let the cat eat out of her plate!" cried Betty.

"And did you see Genevieve's when Mrs. Brewster-Smith had the dessert set down in front of her to serve!"

"How about little Eleanor upsetting the glass of milk on George's trousers!"

"Oh *poor* old George! Did you ever see such gloom!"

Thus bubbling, they came again to Betty's home with the door still open from which she had lately emerged. There Betty fell suddenly silent, all the laughter gone from her face. The man peered in the dusk, apprehensive. What had gone wrong, now, after all?

"Do you know, Penny, we're pigs!" she said suddenly, with energy. "We're hateful, abominable pigs!"

He glared at her and clutched his hair.

"Didn't you see Emelene Brand's face? I can't get it out of my mind! It makes me sick, it was so happy and peaceful and befooled! Poor old dear! She *believes* all that! And she's the only one who does! And it's beastly in us to make a joke of it! She has wanted a home all her life, and she'd have made a lovely one, too, for children! And she's been kept from it by all this fool's talk about womanliness."

"Help! What under the sun are you . . ." began Penfield.

"Why, look here, she's not and never was, the kind any man wants to marry. She wouldn't have liked a real husband, either . . . poor, dear, thin-blooded old child! But she wanted a *home* just the same. Everybody does! And if she had been taught how to earn a decent living, if she hadn't been fooled out of her five senses by that idiotic cant about a man's doing everything for you, or else going without . . . why she'd be working now, a happy, useful woman, bringing up two or three adopted children in a decent home she'd made for them with her own efforts . . . instead of making her loving heart ridiculous over a cat. . . ."

She dashed her hand over her eyes angrily, and stood silent for a moment, trying to control her quivering chin before she went into the house.

The young man touched her shoulder with reverent fingers.

"Betty," he said in a rather unsteady voice, "it's *true,* all that bally-rot about women being better than men. You *are!*"

With which very modern compliment, he turned and left her.

V

BY KATHLEEN NORRIS

HER first evening with her augmented family Genevieve Remington never forgot. It is not at all likely that George ever forgot it, either; but to George it was only one in the series of disturbing events that followed his unqualified repudiation of the suffrage cause.

To Genevieve's tender heart it meant the wreckage, not the preservation of the home; that lovely home to whose occupancy she had so hopefully looked. She was too young a wife to recognize in herself the evanescent emotions of the bride. The blight had fallen upon her for all time. What had been fire was ashes; it was all over. The roseate dream had been followed by a cruel, and a lasting, awakening.

Some day Genevieve would laugh at the memory of this tragic evening, as she laughed at George's stern ultimatums, and at Junior's decision to be an engineer, and at Jinny's tiny cut thumb. But she had no sense of humor now. As she ran to the corner, and poured the whole distressful story into her husband's ears, she felt the walls of her castle in Spain crashing about her ears.

George, of course, was wonderful; he had been that all his life. He only smiled, at first, at her news.

"You poor little sweetheart!" he said to his wife, as she clung to his arm, and they entered the house together. "It's a shame to distress you so, just as we are getting settled, and Marie and Lottie are working in! But it's too absurd, and to have you worry your little head is ridiculous, of course! Let them stay here to dinner, and then I'll just quietly take it for granted that they are going home—"

"But—but their trunks are here, dearest!"

Husband and wife were in their own room now, and Genevieve was rapidly recovering her calm. George turned from his mirror to frown at her in surprise.

"Their trunks! They didn't lose any time, did they? But do you mean to say there was no telephoning—no notice at all?"

"They may have telephoned, George, love. But I was over at Grace Hatfield's for a while, and I got back just before they came in!"

George went on with his dressing, a thoughtful expression on his face. Genevieve thought he looked stunning in the loose Oriental robe he wore while he shaved.

"Well, whatever they think, we can't have this, you know," he said presently. "I'll have to be quite frank with Alys,—of course Emelene has no sense!"

"Yes, be quite frank!" Genevieve urged eagerly. "Tell them that of course you were only speaking figuratively. Nobody ever means that a woman really can't get along without a man's protection, because look at the women who *do*—"

She stopped, a little troubled by the expression on his face.

"I said what I truly believe, dear," he said kindly. "You know that!"

Genevieve was silent. Her heart beat furiously, and she felt that she was going to cry. He was angry with her—he was angry with her! Oh, what had she said, what *had* she said!

"But for all that," George continued, after a moment, "nobody but two women could have put such an idiotic construction upon my words. I am certainly going to make that point with Alys. A sex that can jump headlong to such a perfectly untenable conclusion is very far from ready to assume the responsibilities of citizenship—"

"George, dearest!" faltered Genevieve. She did not want to make him cross again, but she could not in all loyalty leave him under this misunderstanding, to approach the always articulate Alys.

"George, it was Penny, I'm sure!" she said. "From what they said,—they talked all the time!—I think Penny went to see them, and sort of—sort of—suggested this! I'm so sorry, George—"

George was sulphurously silent.

"And Penny will make the most of it, you know!"

Genevieve went on quickly and nervously. "If you should send them back, tonight, I know he'd tell Betty! And Betty says she is coming to see you because she has been asked to read an answer to your paper, at the Club, and she might—she has such a queer sense of humor—"

Silence. Genevieve wished that she was dead, and that every one was dead.

"I don't want to criticize you, dear," George said presently, in his kindest tone. "But the time to *act,* of course, was when they first arrived. I can't do anything now. We'll just have to face it through, for a few days."

It was not much of a cloud, but it was their first. Genevieve went downstairs with tears in her eyes.

She had wanted their home to be so cozy, so dainty, so intimate! And now to have two grown women and a child thrust into her Paradise! Marie was sulky, rattling the silver-drawer viciously while her mistress talked to her, and Lottie had an ugly smile as she submitted respectfully that there wasn't enough asparagus.

Then George's remoteness was terrifying. He carved with appalling courtesy.

"Is there another chicken, Genevieve?" he asked, as if he had only an impersonal interest in her kitchen. No, there was only the one. And plenty, too, said the guests pleasantly. Genevieve hoped there were eggs and bacon for Marie and Lottie and Frieda.

"I'm going to ask you for just a mouthful more, it tastes so delicious and homy!" said Alys. "And then I want to talk a little business, George. It's about those houses of mine, out in Kentwood. . . ."

George looked at her blankly, over his drumstick.

"Darling Tom left them," said Tom's widow, "and they really have rented well. They're right near the factory, you know. But now, just lately, some man from the agents has been writing and writing me; he says that one of them has been condemned, and that unless I do something or other they'll all be condemned. It's a horrid neighborhood, and I don't like the idea, anyway, of a woman poking about among drains and cellars. Yet, if I send the agent, he'll run me into fearful expense; they always do. So I'm going to take them out of his hands tomorrow, and turn it all over to you, and whatever you decide will be best!"

"My dear girl, I'm the busiest man in the world!" George said. "Leave all that to Allen. He's the best agent in town!"

"Oh, I took them away from Allen months ago, George. Sampson has them now."

"Sampson? What the deuce did you change for? I don't know that Sampson is solvent. I certainly would go back to Allen—"

"George, I can't!" The widow looked at her plate, swept him a coquettish glance, and dropped her eyes again.

"Mr. Allen is a dear fellow," she elucidated, "but his wife is dreadful! There's nothing she won't suspect, and nothing she won't say!"

"My dear cousin, this isn't a question of social values! It's business!" George said impatiently. "But I'll tell you what to do," he added, after scowling thought. "You put it in Miss Eliot's hands; she was with Allen for some years. Now she's gone in for herself, and she's doing well. We've given her several things—"

"Take it out of a man's hands to put it into a woman's!" Alys exclaimed. And Emelene added softly:

"What can a woman be thinking of, to go into a dreadful business like selling real estate and collecting rents!"

"Of course, she was trained by men!" Genevieve threw in, a little anxiously. Alys was so tactless, when George was tired and hungry. She cast about desperately for some neutral topic, but before she could find one the widow spoke again.

"I'll tell you what I'll do, George. I'll bring the books and papers to your office tomorrow morning, and then you can do whatever you think best! Just send me a check every month, and it will be all right!"

"Just gather me up what's there, on the plate," Emelene said, with her nervous little laugh in the silence. "I declare I don't know when I've eaten such a dinner! But that reminds me that you could help me out wonderfully, too, Cousin George—I can't quite call you Mr. Remington!—with those wretched stocks of mine.

"I'm sure I don't know what they've been doing, but I know I get less money all the time! It's the New Haven, George, that P'pa left me two years ago. I can't understand anything about it, but yesterday I was talking to a young man who advised me to put all my money into some tonic stock. It's a tonic made just of plain earth—he says it makes everything grow. Doesn't it sound reasonable? But if I should lose all I have, I'm afraid I'd *really* wear my welcome out, Genevieve, dear. So perhaps you'll advise me?"

"I'll do what I can!" George smiled, and Genevieve's heart rose. "But upon my word, what you both tell me isn't a strong argument for Betty's cause!" he added good-naturedly.

"P'pa always said," Emelene quoted, "that if a woman looked about for a man to advise her, she'd find him! And as I sit here now, in this lovely home, I think—isn't it sweeter and wiser and better this way? For a while,—because I was a hot-headed, rebellious girl!—I couldn't see that he was right. I had had a disappointment, you know," she went on, her kind, mild eyes watering. Genevieve, who had been gazing in some astonishment at the once hot-headed, rebellious girl, sighed sympathetically. Every one knew about the Reverend Mr. Totter's death.

"And after that I just wanted to be busy," continued Emelene. "I wanted to be a trained nurse, or a matron, or something! I look back at it now, and wonder what I was thinking about! And then dear Mama went, and I stepped into her place with P'pa. He wasn't exactly an invalid, but he did like to be fussed over, to have his meals cooked by my own hands, even if we were in a hotel. And whist—dear me, how I used to dread those three rubbers every evening! I was only a young woman then, and I suppose I was attractive to other men, but I never forgot Mr. Totter. And Cousin George," she turned to him submissively, "when you were talking about a woman's real sphere, I felt—well, almost guilty. Because only that one man ever asked me. Do you think, feeling as I did, that I should have deliberately made myself attractive to men?"

George cleared his throat.

"All women can't marry, I suppose. It's in England, I believe, that there are a million unmarried women. But you have made a contented and a womanly life for yourself, and, as a matter of fact, there always *has* been a man to stand between you and the struggle!" he said.

"I know. First P'pa, and now you!" Emelene mused happily.

"I wasn't thinking of myself. I was thinking that your father left you a comfortable income!" he said quickly.

"And now you have asked me here; one of the dearest old places in town!" Emelene added innocently.

Genevieve listened in a stupefaction. This was married life, then? Not since her childhood had Genevieve so longed to stamp, to scream, to protest, to tear this twisted scheme apart and start anew!

She was not a crying woman, but she wanted to cry now. She was not—she told herself indignantly—quite a fool. But she felt that if George went on being martyred, and mechanically polite, and grim, she would go into hysterics. She had been married less than six weeks; that night she cried herself to sleep.

Her guests were as agreeable as their natures permitted; but Genevieve was reduced, before the third day of their visit, to a condition of continual tears.

This was her home, this was the place sacred to George and herself, and their love. Nobody in the world,—not his mother, not hers, had their mothers been living!—was welcome here. She had planned to be such a good wife to him, so thoughtful, so helpful, so brave when he must be away. But she could not rise to the height of sharing him with other women, and saying whatever she said to him in the hearing of witnesses. And then she dared not complain too openly! That was an additional hardship, for if George insulted his guests, then that horrid Penny—

Genevieve had always liked Penny, and had danced and flirted with him æons ago. She had actually told Betty that she hoped Betty would marry Penny. But now she felt that she loathed him. He was secretly laughing at George, at George who had dared to take a stand for old-fashioned virtue and the purity of the home!

It was all so unexpected, so hard. Women everywhere were talking about George's article, and expected her to defend it! George, she could have defended. But how could she talk about a subject upon which she was not informed, in which, indeed, as she was rather fond of saying, she was absolutely uninterested?

George was changed, too. Something was worrying him; and it was hard on the darling old boy to come home to Miss Emelene and the cat and Eleanor and Alys, every night! Emelene adored him, of course, and Alys was always interesting and vivacious, but—but it wasn't like coming home to his own little Genevieve!

The bride wept in secret, and grew nervous and timid in manner. Mrs. Brewster-Smith, however, found this comprehensible enough, and one hot summer afternoon Genevieve went into George's office with her lovely head held high, her color quite gone, and her breath coming quickly with indignation.

"George—I don't care what we do, or where we go! But I can't stand it! She said—she said—she told me—"

Her husband was alone in his office, and Genevieve was now crying in his arms. He patted her shoulder tenderly.

"I'm so worried all the time about dinners, and Lottie's going, and that child getting downstairs and letting in flies and licking the frosting off the maple cake," sobbed Genevieve, "that of *course* I show it! And if I *have* given up my gym work, it's just because I was so busy trying to get some one in Lottie's place! And now they say—they say—that *they* know what the matter is, and that I mustn't dance or play golf—the horrible, spying cats! I won't go back, George, I will *not!* I—"

Again George was wonderful. He put his arm about her, and she sat down on the edge of his desk, and leaned against that dear protective shoulder and dried her eyes on one of his monogrammed handkerchiefs. He reminded her of a long-standing engagement for this evening with Betty and Penny, to go out to Sea Light and have dinner and a swim, and drive home in the moonlight. And when she was quiet again, he said tenderly:

"You mustn't let the 'cats' worry you, Pussy. What they think isn't true, and I don't blame you for getting cross! But in one way, dear, aren't they right? Hasn't my little girl been riding and driving and dancing a little too hard? Is it the wisest thing, just now? You have been nervous lately, dear, and excitable. Mightn't there be a reason? Because I don't have to tell you, sweetheart, nothing would make me prouder, and Uncle Martin, of course, has made no secret of how *he* feels! You wouldn't be sorry, dear?"

Genevieve had always loved children deeply. Long before this her happy dreams had peopled the old house in Sheridan Road

It was hard on the darling old boy to come home to Miss Emelene and
the cat and Eleanor and Alys every night.

with handsome, dark-eyed girls, and bright-eyed boys like their father.

But, to her own intense astonishment, she found this speech from her husband distasteful. George would be "proud," and Uncle Martin pleased. But it suddenly occurred to Genevieve that neither George nor Uncle Martin would be tearful and nervous. Neither George nor Uncle Martin need eschew golf and riding and dancing. To be sick, when she had always been so well! To face death, for which she had always had so healthy a horror! Cousin Alex had died when her baby came, and Lois Farwell had never been well after the fourth Farwell baby made his appearance.

Genevieve's tears died as if from flame. She gently put aside the sustaining arm, and went to the little mirror on the wall, to straighten her hat. She remembered buying this hat, a few weeks ago, in the ecstatic last days of the old life.

"We needn't talk of that yet, George," she said quietly.

She could see George's grieved look, in the mirror. There was a short silence in the office.

Then Betty Sheridan, cool in pongee, came briskly in.

"Hello, Jinny!" said she. "Had you forgotten our plan tonight? You're chaperoning me, I hope you realize! I'm rather difficile, too. Genevieve, Pudge is outside; he'll take you out and buy you something cold. I took him to lunch today. It was disgraceful! Except for a frightful-looking mess called German Pot Roast With Carrots and Noodles Sixty, he ate nothing but melon, lemon-meringue pie, and pineapple special. I was absolutely ashamed! George, I would have speech with you."

"Private business, Betty?" he asked pleasantly. "My wife may not have the vote, but I trust her with all my affairs!"

"Indeed, I'm not in the least interested!" Genevieve said saucily.

She knew George was pleased with her as she went happily away.

"It's just as well Jinny went," said Betty, when she and the district-attorney-elect were alone. "Because it's that old bore Colonel Jaynes! He's come again, and he says he *will* see you!"

Deep red rose in George's handsome face.

"He came here last week, and he came yesterday," Betty said, sitting down, "and really I think you should see him! You see, George, in that far-famed article of yours, you remarked that 'a veteran of the civil as well as the Spanish war' had told you that it was the restless outbreaking of a few northern women that helped to precipitate the national catastrophe, and he wants to know if you meant him!"

"I named no names!" George said, with dignity, yet uneasily, too.

"I know you didn't. But you see we haven't many veterans of *both* wars," Betty went on, pleasantly. "And of course old Mrs. Jaynes is a rabid suffragist, and she is simply hopping. He's a mild old man, you know, and evidently he wants to square things with 'Mother.' Now, George, who *did* you mean?"

"A statement like that may be made in a general sense," George remarked, after scowling thought.

"You might have made the statement on your own hook," Betty conceded, "but when you mention an anonymous Colonel, of course they all sit up! He says that he's going to get a signed statement from you that *he* never said that, and publish it!"

"Ridiculous!" said George.

"Then here are two letters," Betty pursued. "One is from the corresponding secretary of the Women's Non-partisan Pacific Coast Association. She says that they would be glad to hear from you regarding your statement that equal suffrage, in the western states, is an acknowledged failure."

"She'll wait!" George predicted grimly.

"Yes, I suppose so. But she's written to our Mrs. Herrington here, asking her to follow up the matter. George, dear," asked Betty maternally, "*why* did you do it? Why couldn't you let well enough alone!"

"What's your other letter?" asked George.

"It's just from Mr. Riker, of the *Sentinel,* George. He wants you to drop in. It seems that they want a correction on one of your statistics about the number of workingwomen in the United States who don't want the vote. He says it only wants a signed line from you that you were mistaken—"

Refusing to see Colonel Jaynes, or to answer the Colonel's letter, George curtly telephoned the editor of the *Sentinel,* and walked home at four o'clock, his cheeks still burning, his mind in a whirl. Big issues should have been absorbing him: and his mind was pestered instead with these midges of the despised cause. Well, it was all in the day's work—

And here was his sweet, devoted wife, fluttering across the hall, as cool as a rose, in her pink and white. And she had packed his things, in case they wanted to spend the night at Sea Light, and the "cats" had gone off for library books, and he must have some ginger-ale, before it was time to go for Betty and Penny.

The day was perfection. The motor-car purred like a racing tiger under George's gloved hand. Betty and Penny were waiting, and the three young persons forgot all differences, and laughed and chatted in the old happy way, as they prepared for the start. But Betty was carrying a book: *Catherine of Russia.*

"Do you know why suffragists should make an especial study of queens, George?" she asked, as she and Penny settled themselves on the back seat.

"Well, I'll be interlocutor," George smiled, glancing up at the house, from which his wife might issue at any moment. "Why should suffragists read the lives of queens, Miss Bones?"

"Because queens are absolutely the only women in all history who had equal rights!" Betty answered impassively. "Do you realize that? The only women whose moral and social and political instincts had full sway!"

"And a sweet use they made of them, sometimes!" said George.

"And who were the great rulers," pursued Betty. "Whose name in English history is like the names of Elizabeth and Victoria, or Matilda or Mary, for the matter of that? Who mended and conserved and built up what the kings tore down and wasted? Who made Russia an intellectual power—"

Again Penny had an odd sense of fear. Were women perhaps superior to men, after all!

"I don't think Catherine of Russia is a woman to whom a lady can point with pride," George said conclusively. Genevieve, who had appeared, shot Betty a triumphant glance as they started.

Pudge waved to them from the candy store at the corner.

"There's a new candy store every week!" said Penny, shuddering. "Heaven help that poor boy; it must be in the blood!"

"Women must always have something sweet to nibble," George said, leaning back. "The United States took in two millions last year in gum alone!"

"Men chew gum!" suggested Betty.

"But come now, Betty, be fair!" George said. "Which sex eats more candy?"

"Well, I suppose women do," she admitted.

"You count the candy stores, down Main Street," George went on, "and ask yourself how it is that these people can pay rents and salaries just on candy,—nothing else. Did you ever think of that?"

"Well, I could vote with a chocolate in my mouth!" Betty muttered mutinously, as the car turned into the afternoon peace of the main thoroughfare.

"You count them on your side, Penny, and I will on mine!" Genevieve suggested. "All down the street."

"Well, wait—we've passed two!" Penny said excitedly.

"Go on; there's three. That grocery store with candy in the window!"

"Groceries don't count!" objected Betty.

"Oh, they do, too! And drug stores . . . Every place that sells candy!"

"Drug stores and groceries and fruit stores only count half a point," Betty stipulated. "Because they sell other things!"

"That's fair enough," George conceded here, with a nod.

Genevieve and Penny almost fell out of the car in their anxiety not to miss a point, and George quite deliberately lingered on the cross-streets, so that the damning total might be increased.

Laughing and breathless, they came to the bridge that led from the town to the open fields, and took the count.

"One hundred and two and a half!" shouted Penny and Genevieve triumphantly. George smiled over his wheel.

"Oh, women, women !" he said.

"One hundred and sixty-one!" said Betty. There was a shout of protest.

"Oh, Betty Sheridan! You didn't! Why, we didn't miss *one!*"

"I wasn't counting candy stores," smiled Betty. "Just to be different, I counted cigar stores and saloons. But it doesn't signify much either way, does it, George?"

VI

BY HENRY KITCHELL WEBSTER

Of the quartette who, an hour later, emerged from the bath-houses and scampered across the satiny beech into a discreetly playful surf, Genevieve was the one real swimmer. She was better even than Penny, and she left Betty and George nowhere.

She had an endless repertory of amphibious stunts which she performed with gusto, and in the intervals she took an equal satisfaction in watching Penny's heroic but generally disastrous attempts to imitate them.

The other two splashed around aimlessly and now and then remonstrated.

Now, it's all very well to talk about two hearts beating as one, and in the accepted poetical sense of the words, of course Genevieve's and George's did. But as a matter of physiological fact, they didn't. At the end of twenty minutes or so George began turning a delicate blue and a clatter as of distant castanets provided an obligato when he spoke, the same being performed by George's teeth.

The person who made these observations was Betty.

"You'd better go out," she said. "You're freezing."

It ought to have been Genevieve who said it, of course, though the fact that she was under water more than half the time might be advanced as her excuse for failing to say it. But who could venture to excuse the downright callous way in which she exclaimed, "Already? Why we've just got in! Come along and dive through that wave. That'll warm you up!"

It was plain to George that she didn't care whether he was cold or not. And, though the idea wouldn't quite go into words, it was also clear to him that an ideal wife—a really womanly wife— would have turned blue just a little before he began to.

"Thanks," he said, in a cold blue voice that matched the color of his finger nails. "I think I've had enough."

Betty came splashing along beside him.

"I'm going out, too," she said. "We'll leave these porpoises to their innocent play."

This was almost pure amiability, because she wasn't cold, and she'd been having a pretty good time. Her other (practically negligible) motive was that Penny might be reminded, by her withdrawal, of his forgotten promise to teach her to float—and be sorry. Altogether, George would have been showing only a natural and reasonable sense of his obligations if he'd brightened up and flirted with her a little, instead of glooming out to sea the way he did, paying simply no attention to her at all. So at last she pricked him.

"Isn't it funny," she said, "the really blighting contempt that swimmers feel for people who can't feel at home in the water— people who gasp and shiver and keep their heads dry?"

She could see that, in one way, this remark had done George good. It helped warm him up. Leaning back on her hands, as she did, she could see the red come up the back of his neck and spread into his ears. But it didn't make him conversationally any more exciting. He merely grunted. So she tried again.

"I suppose," she said dreamily, "that the myth about mermaids must be founded in fact. Or is it sirens I'm thinking about? Perfectly fascinating, irresistible women, who lure men farther and farther out, in the hope of a kiss or something, until they get exhausted and drown. I'll really be glad when Penny gets back alive."

"And I shall be very glad," said George, trying hard for a tone of condescending indifference appropriate for use with one who has played dolls with one's little sister, "I shall really be very glad when you make up your mind what you are going to do with Penny. He's just about a total loss down at the office as it is, and he's getting a worse idiot from day to day. And the worst of it is, I imagine you know all the while what you're going to do about it— whether you're going to take him or not."

The girl flushed at that. He was being almost too outrageously rude, even for George. But before she said anything to that effect, she thought of something better.

"I shall never marry any man," she said very intensely, "whose heart is not with the Cause. You know what Cause I mean, George—the Suffrage Cause. When I see thoughtless girls handing over their whole lives to men who . . ."

It sounded like the beginning of an oration.

"Good Lord!" her victim cried. "Isn't there anything else than that to talk about—*ever?*"

"But just think how lucky you are, George," she said, "that at home they all think exactly as you do!"

He jumped up. Evidently this reminder of the purring acquiescences of Cousin Emelene and Mrs. Brewster-Smith laid no balm upon his harassed spirit.

"You may leave my home alone, if you please."

He was frightfully annoyed, of course, or he wouldn't have said anything as crude as that. In a last attempt to recover his scattered dignity, he caught at his office manner.

"By the way," he said, "you forgot to remind me today to write a letter to that Eliot woman about Mrs. Brewster-Smith's cottages."

With that he stalked away to dress. Genevieve and Penny, now shoreward bound, hailed him. But it wasn't quite impossible to pretend he didn't hear, and he did it.

The dinner afterward at the Sea Light Inn was a rather gloomy affair. George's lonely grandeur was only made the worse, it seemed, by Genevieve's belated concern lest he might have taken cold through not having gone and dressed directly he came out of the water. Genevieve then turned very frosty to Penny, having decided suddenly that it was all his fault.

As for Betty, though she was as amiable a little soul as breathed, she didn't see why she should make any particular effort to console Penny, just because his little flirtation with Genevieve had stopped with a bump.

Even the ride home in the moonlight didn't help much. Genevieve sat beside George on the front seat, and between them there stretched a tense, tragic silence. In the back seat with Penfield Evans, and in the intervals of frustrating his attempts to hold her hand, Betty considered how frightfully silly young married couples could be over microscopic differences.

But Betty was wrong here and the married pair on the front seat were right.

Just reflect for a minute what Genevieve's George was. He was her knight, her Bayard, her thoroughly Tennysonian King Arthur. The basis of her adoration was that he should remain like that. You can see then what a staggering experience it was to have caught herself, even for a minute, in the act of smiling over him as sulky and absurd.

And think of George's Genevieve! A saint enshrined, that his soul could profitably bow down before whenever it had leisure to escape from the activities of a wicked world. Fancy his horror over the mere suspicion that she could be indifferent to his wishes—his comfort—even his health, because of a mere tomboy flirtation with a man who could swim better than he could! Most women were like that, he knew—vain, shallow, inconstant creatures! But was not his pearl an exception? It was horrible to have to doubt it.

By three o'clock the next morning, after many tears and much grave discourse, they succeeded in getting these doubts to sleep— killing them, they'd have said, beyond the possibility of resurrection. It was the others who had made all the trouble. If only they could have the world to themselves—no Cousin Emelene, no Alys Brewster-Smith, no Penfield Evans and Betty Sheridan, with their frivolity and low ideals, to complicate things! An Arcadian Island in some Æonian Sea.

"Well," he said hopefully, "our home can be like that. It shall be like that, when we get rid of Alys and her horrible little girl, and Cousin Emelene and her unspeakable cat. It shall be our world; and no troubles or cares or worries shall ever get in there!"

She acquiesced in this prophecy, but even as she did so, cuddling her face against his own, a lowdown, unworthy spook, whose existence in her he must never suspect, said audibly in her inner ear, "Much he knows about it!"

Betty did not forget to remind George of the letter he was to write to Miss Eliot about taking over the agency of Mrs. Brewster-Smith's cottages. In the composition of this letter George washed his hands of responsibility with, you might say, antiseptic care.

He had taken pleasure in recommending Miss Eliot, he explained, and Mrs. Brewster-Smith was acting on his recommendation. Any questions arising out of the management of the property should be taken up directly with her client. Miss Eliot would have no difficulty in understanding that the enormous pressure of work which now beset him precluded him from having anything more to do with the matter.

The letter was typed and inclosed in a big linen envelope, with the mess of papers Alys had dumped upon his desk a few days previously, and it was despatched forthwith by the office boy.

"There," said George on a note of grim satisfaction, "that's done!"

The grimness lasted, but the satisfaction did not. Or only until the return of the office boy, half an hour later, with the identical envelope and a three-line typewritten note from Miss Eliot. She was sorry to say, she wrote, that she did not consider it advisable to undertake the agency for the property in question. Thanking him, nevertheless, for his courtesy, she was his very truly, E. Eliot.

George summoned Betty by means of the buzzer, and asked her, with icy indignation, what she thought of that. But, as he was visibly bursting with impatience to say what *he* thought of it, she gave him the opportunity.

"I thought you advanced women," he said, "were supposed to stand by each other—stand by all women—try to make things better for them. One for all—all for one. That sort of thing. But it really works the other way. It's just because a woman owns those cottages that Miss Eliot won't have anything to do with them. She knows that women are unreasonable and hard to get on with in business matters, so she passes the buck! Back to a man, if you please, who hasn't any more real responsibility for it than she has."

There was, of course, an obvious retort to this; namely, that business was business, and that a business woman had the same privilege a business man had, of declining a job that looked as if it would entail more bother than it was worth. But Betty couldn't quite bring herself to take this line. Women, if they could ever get the chance (through the vote and in other ways), were going to make the world a better place—run it on a better lot of ideals. It wouldn't do to begin justifying women on the ground that they

were only doing what men did. As well abandon the whole cru-
sade right at the beginning.

George saw her looking rather thoughtful, and pressed his ad-
vantage. Suppose Betty went and saw Miss Eliot personally, sometime today, and urged her to reconsider. The business didn't amount
to much, it was true, and it no doubt involved the adjustment of
some troublesome details. But unless Miss Eliot would undertake
it, he wouldn't know just where to turn. Alys had quarreled with
Allen, and Sampson was a skate. And perhaps a little plain talk to
Alys about the condition of the cottages—"from one of her own
sex," George said this darkly and looked away out of the window at
the time—might be productive of good.

"All right," Betty agreed, "I'll see what I can do. It's kind of
hard to go to a woman you barely know by sight, and talk to her
about her duty, but I guess I'm game. If you can spare me, I'll go
now and get it over with."

There were no frills about Edith Eliot's real estate office,
though the air of it was comfortably busy and prosperous.

The place had once been a store. An architect's presentation of
an apartment building, now rather dusty, occupied the show-window.
There was desk accommodation for two or three of those bright
young men who make a selection of keys and take people about to
look at houses; there was a stenographer's desk with a stenographer
sitting at it; and back of a table in the corner, in the attitude of one
making herself as comfortable as the heat of the day would permit,
while she scowled over a voluminous typewritten document, was
E. Eliot herself. It was almost superfluous to mention that her name
was Edith. She never signed it, and there was no one, in Whitewater anyway, who called her by it.

She was a big-boned young woman (that is, if you call the
middle thirties young), with an intelligent, homely face, which
probably got the attraction some people surprisingly found in it
from the fact that she thought nothing about its looks one way or
the other. It was rather red when Betty came in, and she was making it rapidly redder with the vigorous ministrations of a man's-size
handkerchief.

She greeted Betty with a cordial "how-de-doo," motioned her to the other chair at the table (Betty had a fleeting wish that she might have dusted it before she sat down), and asked what she could do for her.

"I'm from Mr. Remington's office," Betty said, "Remington and Evans. He wrote you a note this morning about some cottages that belong to a cousin of his, Mrs. Brewster-Smith."

"I answered that note by his own messenger," said E. Eliot. "He should have got the reply before this."

"Oh, he got it," said Betty, "and was rather upset about it. What I've come for, is to urge you to reconsider."

E. Eliot smiled rather grimly at her blotting-pad, looked up at Betty, and allowed her smile to change its quality. What she said was not what she had meant to say before she looked up. E. Eliot was always upbraiding herself for being sentimental about youth and beauty in her own sex. She'd never been beautiful, and she'd never been young—not young like Betty. But the upbraidings never did any good.

She said: "I thought I had considered sufficiently when I answered Mr. Remington's note. But it's possible I hadn't. What is it you think I may have overlooked?"

"Why," said Betty, "George thought the reason you wouldn't take the cottages was because a woman owned them. He used it as a sort of example of how women wouldn't stick together. He said that you probably knew that women were unreasonable and hard to deal with and didn't want the bother."

It disconcerted Betty a little that E. Eliot interposed no denial at this point, though she'd paused to give her the opportunity.

"You see," she went on a little breathlessly, "I'm for women suffrage and economic independence and all that. I think it's perfectly wonderful that you should be doing what you are—showing that women can be just as successful in business as men can. Of course I know that you've got a perfect *right* to do just what a man would do—refuse to take a piece of business that wasn't worth while. But—but what we hope is, and what we want to show men is, that when women get into politics and business they'll be better and less selfish."

"Which do you mean will be better?" E. Eliot inquired. "The politics and the business, or the women?"

"I mean the politics and the business," Betty told her rather frostily. Was the woman merely making fun of her? E. Eliot caught the note. "I meant my question seriously," she said. "It has a certain importance. But I didn't mean to interrupt you. Go ahead."

"Well," Betty said, "that's about all. George—Mr. Remington—that is—is running for district attorney, and he has come out against suffrage as you know. I thought perhaps this was a chance to convert him a little. It would be a great favor to him, anyway, if you took the cottages; because he doesn't know whom to turn to, if you won't. I didn't come to try to tell you what your duty is, but I thought perhaps you hadn't just looked at it that way."

"All right," said E. Eliot. "Now I'll tell you how I *do* look at it. In the first place, about doing business for women. It all depends on the woman you're doing business with. If she's had the business training of a man, she's as easy to deal with as a man. If she's never had any business training at all, if business doesn't mean anything to her except some vague hocus-pocus that produces her income, then she's seven kinds of a Tartar.

"She has no more notion about what she has a right to expect from other people, or what they've a right to expect from her, than a white Angora cat. Of course, the majority of women who have property to attend to have had it dumped on their hands in middle life, or after, by the wills of loving husbands. Those women, I'll say frankly, are the devil and all to deal with. But it's their husbands' and fathers' fault, and not their own. Anyhow, that isn't the reason I wouldn't take those cottages.

"It was the cottages themselves, and not the woman who owned them, that decided me. That whole Kentwood district is a disgrace to civilization. The sanitary conditions are filthy; have been for years. The owners have been resisting condemnation proceedings right along, on the ground that the houses brought in so little rental that it would be practical confiscation to compel them to make any improvements. Now, since the war boon struck the mills, and every place with four walls and a roof is full, they're saying they can't afford to make any change because of the frightful loss they'd suffer in potential profits.

"Well, when you agree to act as a person's agent, you've got to act in that person's interest; and when it's a question of the interest of the owners of those Kentwood cottages, whether they're men or women, my idea was that I didn't care for the job."

"I think you're perfectly right about it," Betty said. "I wouldn't have come to urge you to change your mind, if I had understood what the situation was. But," here she held out her hand, "I'm glad I did come, and I wish we might meet again sometime and get acquainted and talk about things."

"No time like the present," said E. Eliot. "Sit down again, if you've got a minute." She added, as Betty dropped back into her chair, "You're Elizabeth Sheridan, aren't you?—Judge Sheridan's daughter? And you're working as a stenographer for Remington and Evans?"

Betty nodded and stammered out the beginning of an apology for not having introduced herself earlier. But the older woman waved this aside.

"What I really want to know," she went on, "if it isn't too outrageous a question, is what on earth you're doing it for—working in that law office, I mean?"

It was a question Betty was well accustomed to answering. But coming from this source, it surprised her into a speechless stare.

"Why," she said at last, "I do it because I believe in economic independence for women. Don't you? But of course you do."

"I don't know," said E. Eliot. "I believe in food and clothes, and money to pay the rent, and the only way I have ever found of having those things was to get out and earn them. But if ever I make money enough to give me an independent income half the size of what yours must be, I'll retire from business in short order."

"Do you know," said Betty, "I don't believe you would. I think you're mistaken. I don't believe a woman like you could live without working."

"I didn't say I'd quit working," said E. Eliot. "I said I'd quit business. That's another thing. There's plenty of real work in the world that won't earn you a living. Lord! Don't I see it going by right here in this office! There are things I just itch to get my hands into, and I have to wait and tell myself 'some day, perhaps!' There's a thing I'd like to do now, and that's to take a hand in this political campaign for district attorney. It would kill my business deader than Pharaoh's aunt, so I've got to let it go. But it would certainly put your friend George Remington up a tall tree."

"Oh, you're a suffragist, then?" Betty exclaimed eagerly. "I was wondering about that. I've never seen you at any of our meetings."

"I'm a suffragist, all right," said E. Eliot, "but as your meetings are mostly held in the afternoons, when I'm pretty busy, I haven't been able to get 'round.

"I'm curious about Remington," she went on. "I've known him a little, for years. When I worked for Allen, I used to see him quite often in the office. And I'd always rather liked him. So that I was surprised, clear down to the ground, when I read that statement of his in the *Sentinel*. I'd never thought he was *that* sort. And from the fact that you work in his office and like him well enough to call him George one might almost suppose he wasn't."

Clearly Betty was puzzled. "Of course," she said, "I think his views about women are obsolete and ridiculous. But I don't see what they've got to do with liking him or not, personally."

E. Eliot's smile became grim again, but she said nothing, so Betty asked a direct question.

"That was what you meant, wasn't it?"

"Yes," the other woman said, "that was what I meant. Why, if you don't mind plain speaking, it's been my observation that the sort of men who think the world is too indecent for decent women to go out into, generally have their own reasons for knowing how indecent it is; and that when they spring a line of talk like that, they're being sickening hypocrites into the bargain."

Betty's face had gone flame color.

"George isn't like that at all," she said. "He's—he's really fine. He's old-fashioned and sentimental about women, but he isn't a hypocrite. He really means those things he says. Why . . ."

And then Betty went on to tell her new friend about Cousin Emelene and Alys Brewster-Smith, and how George, though he writhed, had stood the gaff.

"A grown-up man," E. Eliot summed up, "who honestly believes that women are made of something fine and fragile, and that they ought to be kept where even the wind can't blow upon them! But good heavens, child, if he really means that, it makes it all the better for what I was thinking of. You don't understand, of course. I hadn't meant to tell you, but I've changed my mind.

"Listen now. That statement in the *Sentinel* has set the town talking, of course, and stirred up a lot of feeling, for and against suffrage. But what it would be worth as an issue to go to the mat with on election day, is exactly nothing at all. You go out and ask a voter to vote against a candidate for district attorney because he's an anti-suffragist, and he'll say, 'What difference does it make? It isn't up to him to give women the vote. It doesn't matter to me what his private opinions are, as long as he makes a good district attorney!' But there is an issue that we *can* go to the mat with, and so far it hasn't been raised at all. There hasn't been a peep." She reached over and laid a hand on Betty's arm.

"Do you know what the fire protection laws for factories are? And do you know that it's against the law for women to work in factories at night? Well, and do you know what the conditions are in every big mill in this town? With this boom in war orders, they've simply taken off the lid. Anything goes. The fire and building ordinances are disregarded, and for six months the mills have been running a night shift as well as a day shift, on Sundays and week-days, and three-quarters of their operatives are women. Those women go to work at seven o'clock at night, and quit at six in the morning; and they have an hour off from twelve to one in the middle of the night.

"Now do you see? It's up to the district attorney to enforce the law. Isn't it fair to ask this defender of the home whether he believes that women should be home at night or not, and if he does, what he's going to do about it? Talk about slogans! The situation bristles with them! We could placard this town with a lot of big black-faced questions that would make it the hottest place for George Remington that he ever found himself in.

"Well, it would be pretty good campaign work if he was the hypocrite I took him to be, from his stuff in the *Sentinel*. But if he's on the level, as you think he is, there's a chance—don't you see there's a chance that he'd come out flat-footed for the enforcement of the law? And if he did! . . . Child, can you see what would happen if he *did?*"

Betty's eyes were shining like a pair of big sapphires. When she spoke, it was in a whisper like an excited child.

"I can see a little," she said. "I think I can see. But tell me."

"In the first place," said E. Eliot, "see whom he'd have against him. There'd be the best people, to start with. Most of them are stockholders in the mills. Why, you must be, yourself, in the Jaffry-Bradshaw Company! Your father was, anyway."

Betty nodded.

"You want to be sure you know what it means," the older woman went on. "This thing might cut into your dividends, if it went through."

"I hope it will," said Betty fiercely. "I never realized before that my money was earned like that—by women, girls of my age, standing over a machine all night." She shivered. "And there are some of us, I'm sure," she went on, "who would feel the way I do about it."

"Well,—some," E. Eliot admitted. "Not many, though. And then there are the merchants. These are great times for them— town crammed with people, all making money, and buying right and left. And then there's the labor vote itself! A lot of laboring men would be against him. Their women just now are earning as much as they are. There are a lot of these men—whatever they might say—who'd take good care not to vote for a man who would prevent their daughters from bringing in the fifteen, twenty, or twenty-five dollars a week they get for that night work.

"Well, and who would be with him? Why, the women themselves. The one chance on earth he'd have for election would be to have the women organized and working for him, bringing every ounce of influence they had to bear on their men—on all the men they knew.

"Mind you, I don't believe he could win at that. But, win or lose, he'd have done something. He'd have shown the women that they needed the vote, and he'd have found out for himself—he and the other men who believe in fair human treatment for everybody—that they can't secure that treatment without women's votes. That's the real issue. It isn't that women are better than men, or that they could run the world better if they got the chance. It's that men and women have got to work together to do the things that need doing."

"You're perfectly wonderful," said Betty, and sat thereafter, for perhaps a minute and a half, in an entranced silence.

Then, with a shake of the head, a straightening of the spine, and a good, deep, business-like preliminary breath, she turned to her new friend and said, "Well, shall we do it?"

This time it was E. Eliot's turn to gasp.

She hadn't expected to have a course of action put up to her in that instantaneous and almost casual manner. She wasn't young like Betty. She'd been working hard ever since she was seventeen years old. She'd succeeded, in a way, to be sure. But her success had taught her how hard success is to obtain. She saw much farther into the consequences of the proposed campaign than Betty could see. She realized the bitter animosity that it would provoke. She knew it was well within the probabilities that her business would be ruined by it.

She sat there silent for a while, her face getting grimmer and grimmer all the time. But she turned at last and looked into the eager face of the girl beside her, and she smiled,—though even the smile was grim.

"All right," she said, holding out her hand to bind the bargain. "We'll start and we'll stick. And here's hoping! We'd better lunch together, hadn't we?"

VII

BY ANNE O'HAGAN

MR. BENJAMIN DOOLITTLE, by profession Whitewater's leading furniture dealer and funeral director, and by the accident of political fortune the manager of Mr. George Remington's campaign, sat in his candidate's private office, and from time to time restrained himself from hasty speech by the diplomatic and dexterous use of a quid of tobacco.

He found it difficult to preserve his philosophy in the face of George Remington's agitation over the woman's suffrage issue.

"It's the last time," he had frequently informed his political cronies since the opening of the campaign, "that I'll wet-nurse a new-fledged candidate. They've got at least to have their milk teeth through if they want Benjamin Doolittle after this."

To George, itchingly aware through all his rasped nerves of Mrs. Herrington's letter in that morning's *Sentinel* asking him to refute, if he could, an abominable half column of statistics in regard to legislation in the Woman Suffrage States, the furniture dealer was drawling pacifically:

"Now, George, you made a mistake in letting the women get your goat. Don't pay no attention to them. Of course their game's fair enough. I will say that you gave them their opening; stood yourself for a target with that statement of yours. Howsomever, you ain't obligated to keep on acting as the nigger head in the shooting gallery.

"Let 'em write; let 'em ask questions in the papers; let 'em heckle you on the stump. All that you've got to say is that you've expressed your personal convictions already, and that you've stood by those convictions in your private life, and that as you ain't up for legislator, the question don't really concern your candidacy. And that, as you're running for district attorney, you will, with their kind permission, proceed to the subjects that do concern you there—the condition of the court calendar of Whitewater County, the prosecution of the racetrack gamblers out at Erie Oval, and so forth, and so forth.

"You laid yourself open, George, but you ain't obligated in law or equity to keep on presenting yourself bare chest for their outrageous slings and arrows."

"Of course, what you say about their total irrelevancy is quite true," said George, making the concession so that it had all the belligerency of a challenge. "But of course I would never have consented to run for office at the price of muzzling my convictions."

Mr. Doolittle wearily agreed that that was more than could be expected from any candidate of the high moral worth of George Remington. Then he went over a list of places throughout the county where George was to speak during the next week, and intimated dolefully that the committee could use a little more money, if it had it.

He expressed it thus: "A few more contributions wouldn't put any strain to speak of on our pants' pockets. Anything more to be got out of Old Martin Jaffry? Don't he realize that blood's thicker than water?"

"I'll speak to him," growled George.

He hated Mr. Benjamin Doolittle's colloquialisms, though once he had declared them amusing, racy, of the soil, and had rebuked Genevieve's fastidious criticisms of them on an occasion when she had interpreted her rôle of helpmeet to include that of hostess to Mr. and Mrs. Doolittle—oh, not in her own home, of course!—at luncheon, at the Country Club!

"Well, I guess that's about all for today."

Mr. Doolittle brought the conference to a close, hoisting himself by links from his chair.

"It takes $3000 every time you circularize the constituency, you know—"

He lounged toward the window and looked out again upon the pleasant, mellow scene around Fountain Square. And with the look his affectation of bucolic calm dropped from him. He turned abruptly.

"What's that going on at McMonigal's corner?" he demanded sharply.

"I don't know, I am sure," said George, with indifference, still bent upon teaching his manager that he was a free and independent citizen, in leading strings to no man. "It's been vacant since the fire in March, when Petrosini's fish market and Miss Letterblair's hat st—"

He had reached the window himself by this time, and the sentence was destined to remain forever unfinished.

From the low, old-fashioned brick building on the northeast corner of Fountain Square, whose boarded eyes had stared blindly across toward the glittering orbs of its towering neighbor, the Jaffry Building, for six months, a series of great placards flared.

Planks had been removed from the windows, plate glass restored, and behind it he read in damnable irritation:

"Some Questions for Candidate Remington."

A foot high, an inch broad, black as Erebus, the letters shouted at him against an orange background.

Every window of the second story contained a placard. On the first story, in the show window where Petrosini had been wont to ravish epicurean eyes by shad and red snapper, perch and trout, cunningly imbedded in ice blocks upon a marble slab—in that window, framed now in the hated orange and black, stood a woman.

She was turning backward, for the benefit of onlookers who pressed close to the glass, the leaves of a mammoth pad resting upon an easel.

From their point of vantage in the second story of the Jaffry Building, the candidate and his manager could see that each sheet bore that horrid headline:

"Questions for Candidate Remington."

The whole population of Whitewater, it seemed to George, was crowded about that corner.

"I'll be back in a minute," said Benjie Doolittle, disappearing through the private office door with the black tails of his coat achieving a true horizontal behind him. As statesman and as un-dertaker, Mr. Doolittle never swerved from the garment which keeps green the memory of the late Prince Consort.

As the door opened, the much-tried George Remington had a glimpse of that pleasing industrial unit, Betty Sheridan, searching through the file for the copy of the letter to the Cummunipaw Steel Works, which he had recently demanded to see. He pressed the buzzer imperiously, and Betty responded with duteous haste. He pointed through the window to the crowd in front of Mc-Monigal's block.

"Perhaps," he said, with what seemed to him Spartan self-re-straint, "*you* can explain the meaning of that scene."

Betty looked out with an air of intelligent interest.

"Oh yes!" she said vivaciously. "I think I can. It's a Voiceless Speech."

"A voice l—" George's own face was a voiceless speech as he repeated two syllables of his stenographer's explanation.

"Yes. Don't you know about voiceless speeches? It's antiquated to try to run any sort of a campaign without them nowadays."

"Perhaps you also know who that—female—" again George's power of utterance failed him. Betty came closer to the window and peered out.

"It's Frances Herrington who is turning the leaves now," she said amiably. "I know her by that ducky toque."

"Frances Herrington! What Harvey Herrington is thinking of to allow—" George's emotion constrained him to broken utter-ance. "And we're dining there tonight! She has no sense of the de-cencies—the—the—the hospitality of existence. We won't go— I'll telephone Genevieve—"

"Fie, fie Georgie!" observed Betty. "Why be personal over a mere detail of a political campaign?"

But before George could tell her why his indignation against his prospective hostess was impersonal and unemotional, the long figure of Mr. Doolittle again projected itself upon the scene.

Betty effaced herself, gliding from the inner office, and George turned a look of inquiry upon his manager.

"Well?" the monosyllable had all the force of profanity.

"Well, the women, durn them, have brought suffrage into your campaign."

"How?"

"How? They've got a list of every blamed law on the statute books relating to women and children, and they're asking on that sheet of leaves over there, if you mean to proceed against all who are breaking those laws here in Whitewater County. And right opposite your own office! It's—it's damn smart. You ought to have got that Herrington woman on your committee."

"It's indelicate, unwomanly, indecent. It shows into what unsexed degradation politics will drag woman. But I'm relieved that that's all they're asking. Of course, I shall enforce the law for the protection of every class in our community with all the power of the—"

"Oh, shucks! There's nobody here but me—you needn't unfurl Old Glory," counseled Mr. Doolittle, a trifle impatiently. "They're asking real questions, not blowing off hot-air. Oh, I say, who owns McMonigal's block since the old man died? We'll have the owner stop this circus. That's the first thing to do."

"I'll telephone Allen. He'll know."

Allen's office was very obliging and would report on the ownership on McMonigal's block in ten minutes.

Mr. Doolittle employed the interval in repeating to George some of the "Questions for Candidate Remington," illegible from George's desk.

"You believe that 'WOMAN'S PLACE IS IN THE HOME.' Will you enforce the law against woman's night work in the factories? Over nine hundred women of Whitewater County are doing night work in the munition plants of Airport, Whitewater and Ondegonk. What do you mean to do about it?"

"You 'DESIRE TO CONSERVE THE THREATENED FLOWER OF WOMANHOOD.'"

A critical listener would have caught a note of ribald scorn in Mr. Doolittle's drawl, as he quoted from his candidate's statement, via the voiceless speech placards.

"To conserve the threatened flower of womanhood, the grape canneries of Omega and Onicrom Townships are employing children of five and six years in defiance of the Child Labor Law of this State. Are you going to proceed against them?"

"'WOMAN IS MAN'S RAREST HERITAGE.' Do you think man ought to burn her alive? Remember the Livingston Loomis-Ladd collar factory fire—fourteen women killed, forty-eight maimed. In how many of the factories in Whitewater, in which women work, are the fire laws obeyed? Do you mean to enforce them?"

The telephone interrupted Mr. Doolittle's hateful litany.

Allen's bright young man begged to report that McMonigal's block was held in fee simple by the widow of the late Michael Mc-Monigal.

Mr. Doolittle juggled the leaves of the telephone directory with the dazzling swiftness of a Japanese ball thrower, and in a few seconds he was speaking to the relict of the late Michael.

George watched him with fevered eyes, listened with fevered ears. The conversation, it was easy to gather, did not proceed as Mr. Doolittle wished.

"Oh! in entire charge—E. Eliot. Oh! In sympathy yourself. Oh, come now, Mrs. McMonigal—"

But Mrs. McMonigal did not come now. The campaign manager frowned as he replaced the receiver.

"Widow owns the place. That Eliot woman is the agent. The suffrage gang has the owner's permission to use the building from now on to election. She says she's in sympathy. Well, we'll have to think of something—"

"It's easy enough," declared George. "I'll simply have a set of posters printed answering their questions. And we'll engage sandwich men to carry them in front of McMonigal's windows. Certainly I mean to enforce the law. I'll give the order to the *Sentinel* press now for the answers—definite, dignified answers."

"See here, George." Mr. Doolittle interrupted him with unusual weightiness of manner. "It's too far along in the campaign for you to go flying off on your own. You've got to consult your managers. This is your first campaign; it's my thirty-first. You've got to take advice—"

"I will not be muzzled."

"Shucks! Who wants to muzzle anybody! But you can't say

everything that's inside of you, can you? There's got to be some choosing. We've got to help you choose.

"The silly questions the women are displaying over there— you can't answer 'em in a word or in two words. This city is having a boom; every valve factory in the valley, every needle and pinfactory, is makin' munitions today—valves and needles and pins all gone by the board for the time being. Money's never been so plenty in Whitewater County and this city is feelin' the benefits of it. People are buying things—clothes, flour, furniture, victrolas, automobiles, rum.

"There ain't a merchant of any description in this county but his business is booming on account of the work in the factories. You can't antagonize the whole population of the place. Why, I dare say, some of your own money and Mrs. Remington's is earning three times what it was two years ago. The First National Bank has just declared a fifteen per cent. dividend, and Martin Jaffry owns fifty-four per cent. of the stock.

"You don't want to put brakes on prosperity. It ain't decent citizenship to try it. It ain't neighborly. Think of the lean years we've known. You can't do it. This war won't last forever—" Mr. Doolittle's voice was tinged with regret—"and it will be time enough to go in for playing the deuce with business when business gets slack again. That's the time for reforms, George,—when things are dull."

George was silent, the very presentment of a sorely harassed young man. He had not, even in a year when blamelessness rather than experience was his party's supreme need in a candidate, become its banner bearer without possessing certain political apperceptions. He knew, as Benjie Doolittle spoke, that Benjie spoke the truth—Whitewater city and county would never elect a man who had too convincingly promised to interfere with the prosperity of the city and county.

"Better stick to the gambling out at Erie Oval, George," counseled the campaign manager. "They're mostly New Yorkers that are interested in that, anyway."

"I'll not reply without due consideration and—er—notice," George sullenly acceded to his manager and to necessity. But he hated both Doolittle and necessity at the moment.

That sun-bright vision of himself which so splendidly and sustainingly companioned him, which spoke in his most sonorous periods, which so completely and satisfyingly commanded the reverence of Genevieve—that George Remington of his brave imaginings would not thus have answered Benjamin Doolittle. Through the silence following the furniture man's departure, Betty, at the typewriter, clicked upon Georgie's ears. An evil impulse assailed him—impolitic, too, as he realized—impolitic but irresistible.

It was the easiest way in which candidate Remington, heckled by suffragists, overridden by his campaign committee, mortifyingly tormented by a feeling of inadequacy, could re-establish himself in his own esteem as a man of prompt and righteous decisions.

He might not be able to run his campaign to suit himself, but, by Jove, his office was his own!

He went into Betty's quarters and suggested to her that a due sense of the eternal fitness of things would cause her to offer him her resignation, which his own sense of the eternal fitness of things would lead him at once to accept.

It seemed, he said, highly indecorous of her to remain in the employ of Remington and Evans the while she was busily engaged in trying to thwart the ambitions of the senior partner. He marveled that woman's boasted sensitiveness had not already led her to perceive this for herself.

For a second, Betty seemed startled, even hurt. She colored deeply and her eyes darkened. Then the flush of surprise and the wounded feeling died. She looked at him blankly and asked how soon it would be possible for him to replace her. She would leave as soon as he desired.

In her bearing, so much quieter than usual, in the look in her face, George read a whole volume. He read that up to this time, Betty had regarded her presence in the ranks of his political enemies as she would have regarded being opposed to him in a tennis match. He read that he, with that biting little speech which he already wished unspoken, had given her a sudden, sinister illumination upon the relations of working women to their employers.

He read the question in the back of her mind. Suppose (so it ran in his constructive fancy) that instead of being a prosperous, protected young woman playing the wage-earner more or less as Marie Antoinette had played the milkmaid, she had been Mamie Riley across the hall, whose work was bitter earnest, whose earnings were not pin money, but bread and meat and brother's schooling and mother's health—would George still have made the stifling of her views the price of her position?

And if George—George, the kind, friendly, clean-minded man would drive that bargain, what bargain might not other men, less gentle, less noble, drive?

All this George's unhappily sensitized conscience read into Betty Sheridan's look, even as the imp who urged him on bade him tell her that she could leave at her own convenience; at once, if she pleased; the supply of stenographers in Whitewater was adequately at demand.

He rather wished that Penny Evans would come in; Penny would doubtless take a high hand with him concerning the episode, and there was nothing which George Remington would have welcomed like an antagonist of his own size and sex.

But Penny did not appear, and the afternoon passed draggingly for the candidate for the district attorneyship. He tried to busy himself with the affairs of his clients, but even when he could keep away from his windows he was aware of the crowds in front of Mc-Monigal's block, of Frances Herrington, her "ducky" toque and her infernal voiceless speech.

And when, for a second, he was able to forget these, he heard from the outer office the unmistakable sounds of a desk being permanently cleared of its present incumbent's belongings.

After a while, Betty bade him a too courteous good-by, still with that abominable new air of gravely readjusting her old impressions of him. And then there was nothing to do but to go home and make ready for dinner at the Herrington's, unless he could induce Genevieve to have an opportune headache.

Of course Betty had been right. Not upon his masculine shoulders should there be laid the absurd burden of political chagrin strong enough to break a social engagement.

Genevieve was in her room. The library was given over to Alys Brewster-Smith, Cousin Emelene Brand, two rusty callers and the tea things. Before the drawing-room fire, Hanna slept in Maltese proprietorship. George longed with passion to kick the cat.

Genevieve, as he saw through the open door, sat by the window. She had, it appeared, but recently come in. She still wore her hat and coat; she had not even drawn off her gloves. And seeing her thus, absorbed in some problem, George's sense of his wrongs grew greater.

He had, he told himself, hurried home out of the jar and fret of a man's day to find balm, to feel the cool fingers of peace pressed upon hot eyelids, to drink strengthening draughts of refreshment from his wife's unquestioning belief, from the completeness of her absorption in him. And here she sat thinking of something else!

Genevieve arose, a little startled as he snapped on the lights and grunted out something which optimism might translate into an affectionate husbandly greeting. She came dutifully forward and raised her face, still exquisite and cool from the outer air, for her lord's home-coming kiss. That resolved itself into a slovenly peck.

"Been out?" asked George unnecessarily. He tried to quell the unreasonable inclination to find her lacking in wifely devotion because she had been out.

"Yes. There was a meeting at the Woman's Forum this afternoon," she answered. She was unpinning her hat before the pier glass, and in it he could see the reflection of her eyes turned upon his image with a questioning look.

"The ladies seem to be having a busy day of it."

He struggled not quite successfully to be facetious over the pretty, negligible activities of his wife's sex. "What mighty theme engaged your attention?"

"That Miss Eliot—the real estate woman, you know—" George stiffened into an attitude of close attention—"spoke about the conditions under which women are working in the mills in this city and in the rest of the county—" Genevieve averted her mirrored eyes from his mirrored face. She moved toward her dressing-table.

"Oh, she, did! and is the Woman's Forum going to come to grips with the industrial monster and bring in the millennium by the first of the year?"

But George was painfully aware that light banter which fails to be convincingly light is but a snarl.

Genevieve colored slightly as she studied the condition of a pair of long white gloves which she had taken from a drawer.

"Of course the Woman's Forum is only for discussion," she said mildly. "It doesn't initiate any action." Then she raised her eyes to his face and George felt his universe reel about him.

For his wife's beautiful eyes were turned upon him, not in limpid adoration, not in perfect acceptance of all his views, unheard, unweighed; but with a question in their blue depths.

The horrid clairvoyance which harassment and self-distrust had given him that afternoon enabled him, he thought, to translate that look. The Eliot woman, in her speech before the Woman's Forum, had doubtless placed the responsibility for the continuation of those factory conditions upon the district attorney's office, had doubtless repeated those damn fool, impractical questions which the suffragists were displaying in McMonigal's windows.

And Genevieve was asking them in her mind! Genevieve was questioning him, his motives, his standards, his intentions! Genevieve was not intellectually a charming mechanical doll who would always answer "yes" and "no" as he pressed the strings, and maintain a comfortable vacuity when he was not at hand to perform the kindly act. Genevieve was thinking on her own account.

What, he wondered angrily, as he dressed—for he could not bring himself to ask her aid in escaping the Herringtons and, indeed, was suddenly balky at the thought of the intimacies of a domestic evening—*what* was she thinking? She was not such an imbecile as to be unaware how large a share of her comfortable fortune was invested in the local industry. Why, her father had been head of the Livingston Loomis-Ladd Collar Company, when that dreadful fire—! And she certainly knew that his uncle, Martin Jaffry, was the chief stockholder in the Jaffry-Bradshaw Company.

What was the question in Genevieve's eyes? Was she asking if he were the knight of those women who worked and sweated and burned, or of her and the comfortable women of her class, of Alys Brewster-Smith with her little cottages, of Cousin Emelene with her little stocks, of masquerading Betty Sheridan whose sortie of independence was from the safe vantage-grounds of entrenched privilege?

And all that evening as he watched his wife across the crystal and the roses of the Herrington table, trying to interpret the question that had been in her eyes, trying to interpret her careful silence, he realized what every husband sooner or later awakes to realize—that he had married a stranger.

He did not know her. He did not know what ambitions, what aspirations apart from him, ruled the spirit behind that charming surface of flesh.

Of course she was good, of course she was tender, of course she was high-minded! But how wide-enveloping was the cloak of her goodness? How far did her tenderness reach out? Was her high-mindedness of the practical or impractical variety?

From time to time, he caught her eyes in turn upon him, with that curious little look of re-examination in their depths. She could look at him like that! She could look at him as though appraisals were possible from a wife to a husband!

They avoided industrial Whitewater County as a topic when they left the Herrington's. They talked with great animation and interest of the people at the party. Arrived at home, George, pleading press of work, went down into the library while Genevieve went to bed. Carefully they postponed the moment of making articulate all that, remaining unspoken, might be ignored.

It was one o'clock and he had not moved a paper for an hour, when the library door opened.

Genevieve stood there. She had sometimes come before when he had worked at night, to chide him for neglecting sleep, to bring bouillon or chocolate. But tonight she did neither.

She did not come far into the room, but standing near the door and looking at him with a new expression—patient, tender, the everlasting eternal look she said: "I couldn't sleep, either. I came down to say something, George. Don't interrupt me—" for he was coming toward her with sounds of affectionate protest at her being out of bed. "Don't speak! I want to say—whatever you do, whatever you decide—now—always—I love you. Even if I don't agree, I love you."

She turned and went swiftly away.

George stood looking at the place where she had stood,—this strange, new Genevieve, who, promising to love, reserved the right to judge.

VIII

BY MARY HEATON VORSE

THE high moods of night do not always survive the clear, cold light of day. Indeed it requires the contribution of both man and wife to keep a high mood in married life.

Genevieve had gone in to make her profession of faith to her husband in a mood which touched the high altitudes. She had gone without any conscious expectation of anything from him in the way of response. She had vaguely but confidingly expected him to live up to the moment.

She had expected something beautiful, a lovely flower of the spirit—comprehension, generosity. Living up to the demand of the moment was George's forte. Indeed, there were those among his friends who felt that there were moments when George lived up to things too brightly and too beautifully. His Uncle Jaffry, for instance, had his openly skeptical moments. But George even lived up to his uncle's skepticism. He accepted his remarks with charming good humor. It was his pride that he could laugh at himself.

At the moment of Genevieve's touching speech he lived up to exactly nothing. He didn't even smile. He only stared at her—a stare which said:

"Now what the devil do you mean by that?"

Genevieve had a flicker of bitter humor when she compared her moment of sentiment to a toy balloon pulled down from the blue by an unsympathetic hand.

The next morning, while George was still shaving, the telephone rang. It was Betty.

"Can you have lunch with me at Thorne's, where we can talk?" she asked Genevieve. "And give me a little time tomorrow afternoon?"

"Why," Genevieve responded, "I thought you were a working girl."

There was a perceptible pause before Betty replied.

"Hasn't George told you?"

"Told what?" Genevieve inquired. "George hasn't told me anything."

"I've left the office."

"Left! For heaven's sake, why?"

Betty's mind worked swiftly.

"Better treat it as a joke," was her decision. There was no pause before she answered.

"Oh, trouble with the boss."

"You'll get over it. You're always having trouble with Penny."

"Oh," said Betty, "it's not with Penny this time."

"Not with George?"

"Yes, with George," Betty answered. "Did you think one couldn't quarrel with the noblest of his sex? Well, one can."

"Oh, Betty, I'm sorry." Genevieve's tone was slightly reproachful.

"Well, I'm not," said Betty. "I like my present job better. It was a good thing he fired me."

"*Fired* you! George fired *you?*"

"Sure thing," responded Betty blithely. "I can't stand here talking all day. What I want to know is, can I see you at lunch?"

"Yes—why, yes, of course," said Genevieve, dazedly. Then she hung up the receiver and stared into space.

George, beautifully dressed, tall and handsome, now emerged from his room. For once his adoring wife failed to notice that in appearance he rivaled the sun god. She had one thing she wanted to know, and she wanted to know it badly. It was,

"Why did you fire Betty Sheridan?"

She asked this in the insulting "point of the bayonet" tone which angry equals use to one another the world over.

Either question or tone would have been enough to have put George's already sensitive nerves on edge. Both together were unbearable. It was, when you came down to it, the most awkward question in the world.

Why, indeed, had he fired Betty Sheridan? He hadn't really given himself an account of the inward reasons yet. The episode had been too disturbing; and it was George's characteristic to put off looking on unpleasant facts as long as possible. Had he been really hard up, which he never had been, he would undoubtedly have put away, unopened, the bills he couldn't pay. Life was already presenting him with the bill of yesterday's ill humor, and he was not yet ready to add up the amount. He hid himself now behind the austerity of the offended husband.

"My dear," he inquired in his turn, "don't you think that you had best leave the details of my office to me?"

He knew how lame this was, and how inadequate before Genevieve replied.

"Betty Sheridan is not a detail of your office. She's one of my best friends, and I want to know why you fired her. I dare say she was exasperating; but I can't see any reason why you should have done it. You should have let her leave."

It was Betty, with that lamentable lack of delicacy which George had pointed out to her, who had not been ready to leave.

"You will have to let me be the judge of what I should or should not have done," said George.

This piece of advice Genevieve ignored.

"Why did you send her away?" she demanded.

"I sent her away, if you want to know, for her insolence and her damned bad taste. If you think—working in my office as she was— it's decent or proper on her part to be active in a campaign that is against me—"

"You mean because she's a suffragist? You sent her away for *that!* Why, really, that's *tyranny!* It's like my sending away some one working for me for her beliefs—"

They stood staring at each other, not questioningly as they had yesterday, but as enemies,—the greater enemies that they so loved each other.

Because of that each word of unkindness was a doubled-edged sword. They quarreled. It was the first time that they had seen each other without illusion. They had been to each other the ideal, the lover, husband, wife.

Now, in the dismay of his amazement in finding himself quarreling with the perfect wife, a vagrant memory came to George that he had heard that Genevieve had a hot temper.

She certainly had. He didn't notice how handsome she looked kindled with anger. He only knew that the rose garden in which they lived was being destroyed by their angry hands; that the very foundation of the life they had been leading was being undermined.

The time of mirage and glamour was over. He had ceased being a hero and an ideal, and why? Because, forgetting his past life, his record, his achievement, Genevieve obstinately insisted on identifying him with one single mistake. He was willing to concede it was a mistake. She had not only identified him with it, but she had called him a number of wounding things.

"Tyrant" was the least of them, and, worse than that, she had, in a very fury of temper, told him that he "needn't take that pompous"—yes, "pompous" had been her unpleasant word—"tone" with her, when he had inquired, more in sorrow than in anger, if this were really his Genevieve speaking.

There was a pause in their hostilities. They looked at each other aghast. Aghast, they had perceived the same awful truth. Each saw that love in the other's heart was dead, and that things never could be the same again. So they stood looking down this dark gulf, and the light of anger died.

In a toneless voice: "We mustn't let Cousin Emelene and Alys hear us quarreling," said George. And Genevieve answered, "They've gone down to breakfast."

The two ladies were seated at table.

"We heard you two love birds cooing and billing, and thought we might as well begin," said Alys Brewster-Smith. "Regularity is of the highest importance in bringing up a child."

Cousin Emelene was reading the *Sentinel*. George's quick eye glanced at the headlines:

Candidate Remington Heckled by Suffragists. Ask Him Leading Questions.

"Why, dear me," she remarked, her kind eyes on George, "it's perfectly awful, isn't it, that they break the laws that way just for a

"You mean because she's a suffragist? You sent her away for t*hat?*
Why, really, that's *tyranny!*"

little more money. But I don't see why they want to annoy dear
George. They ought to be glad they are going to get a district attorney who'll put all those things straight. I think it's very silly of
them to ask him, don't you, Genevieve?"

"Let me see," said Genevieve, taking the paper.

"All he's got to do, anyway, is to answer," pursued Cousin
Emelene.

"Yes, that's all," replied Genevieve, her melancholy gaze on
George. Yesterday she would have had Emelene's childlike faith.
But this stranger, who, for a trivial and tyrannical reason, had sent
away Betty—how would *he* act?

"They showed these right opposite your windows?" she questioned.

"Yes," he returned. "Our friend Mrs. Herrington did it herself. It
was the first course of our dinner. If you think that's good taste—"

"I would expect it of her," said Alys Brewster-Smith.

"But it makes it so easy for George," Emelene repeated.
"They'll know now what sort of a man he is. Little children at
work, just to make a little more money—it's awful!"

"Talking about money, George," said Alys, "have you seen to
my houses yet?"

"Not yet," replied the harassed George. "You'll have to excuse
my going into the reasons now. I'm late as it is."

His voice had not the calm he would have wished for. As he
took his departure, he heard Alys saying,

"If you'll let me, my dear, I'd adore helping you about the
housekeeping. I don't want to stay here and be a burden. If you'll
just turn it over to me, I could cut your housekeeping expenses in
half."

"Damn the women," was the unchivalrous thought that rose to
George's lips.

One would have supposed that trouble had followed closely
enough on George Remington's trail, but now he found it await-
ing him in his office.

Usually, Penny was the late one. It was this light-hearted young
man's custom to blow in with so engaging an expression and so
cheerful a manner that any comment on his unpunctuality was im-

possible. Today, instead of a gay-hearted young man, he looked more like a sentencing judge.

What he wanted to know was,

"What have you done to Betty Sheridan? Do you mean to say that you had the nerve to send her away, send her out of my office without consulting me—and for a reason like that? How did you think I was going to feel about it?"

"I didn't think about you," said George.

"You bet you didn't. You thought about number one and your precious vanity. Why, if one were to separate you from your vanity, one couldn't see you when you were going down the street. Go on, make a frock coat gesture! Play the brilliant but outraged young district attorney. Do you know what it was to do a thing of that kind—to fire a girl because she didn't agree with you?"

"It wasn't because she didn't agree with me," George interrupted, with heat.

"It was the act of a cad," Penny finished. "Look here, young man, I'm going to tell you a few plain truths about yourself. You're not the sort of person that you think you are. You've deceived yourself the way other people are deceived about you—by your exterior. But inside of that good-looking carcass of yours there's a brain composed of cheese. You weren't only a cad to do it—you were a fool!"

"You can't use that tone to me!" cried George.

"Oh, can't I just? By Jove, it's things like that that make one wake up. Now I know why women have a passion for suffrage. I never knew before," Penny went on, with more passion than logic. "You had a nerve to make that statement of yours. You're a fine example of chivalry. You let loose a few things when you wrote that fool statement, but you did a worse trick when you fired Betty Sheridan. God, you're a pinhead—from the point of view of mere tactics. Sometimes I wonder whether you've *any* brain."

George had turned white with anger.

"That'll just about do," he remarked.

"Oh, no, it won't," said Penny. "It won't do at all. I'm not going to remain in a firm where things like this can happen. I wouldn't risk my reputation and my future. You're going to do the decent thing. You're going to Betty Sheridan and tell her what you think of yourself. She won't come back, I suppose, but you might ask her to do that, too. And now I'm going out, to give you time to think this over. And tonight you can tell me what you've decided. And then I'll tell you whether I'm going to dissolve our partnership. Your temper's too bad to decide now. Maybe when you've done that she won't treat me like an unsavory stranger."

He left, and George sat down to gloomy reflection.

To do him justice, the idea of apologizing to Betty had already occurred to him. If he put off the day of reckoning, when the time came he would pay handsomely. He realized that there was no use in wasting energy and being angry with Penny. He looked over the happenings of the last few hours and the part he had played in them, and what he saw failed to please him. He saw himself being advised by Doolittle to concentrate on the Erie Oval. He heard him urging him not to be what Doolittle called unneighborly. The confiding words of Cousin Emelene rang in his ears.

He saw himself, in a fit of ill-temper, discharging Betty. He saw Genevieve, lovely and scornful, urging him to be less pompous. All this, he had to admit, he had brought on himself. Why should he have been so angry at these questions? Again Emelene's remark echoed in his ear. He had only to answer them—and he was going to concentrate on the Erie Oval!

There came a knock on the door, and a breezy young woman demanded,

"D'you want a stenographer?"

George wanted a stenographer, and wanted one badly. He put from him the whole vexed question in the press of work, and by lunch time he made up his mind to have it out with Betty. There was no use putting it off, and he knew that he could have no peace with himself until he did. He felt very tired—as though he had been doing actual physical work. He thought of yesterday as a land of lost content. But he couldn't find Betty.

He bent his steps toward home, and as he did so affection for Genevieve flooded his heart. He so wanted yesterday back—things as they had been. He so wanted her love and her admiration. He wanted to put his tired head on her shoulder. He couldn't bear, not for another moment, to be at odds with her.

He wondered what she had been doing, and how she had spent the morning. He imagined her crying her heart out. He leaped up the steps and ran up to his room. In it was Alys Brewster-Smith. She started slightly.

"I was just looking for some cold cream," she explained.

"Where's Genevieve?" George asked.

"Oh, she's out," Alys replied casually. "She left a note for you."

The note was a polite and noncommittal line informing George that Genevieve would not be back for lunch. He felt as though a lump of ice replaced his heart. His disappointment was the desperate disappointment of a small boy.

He went back to the gloomy office and worked through the interminable day. Late in the afternoon Mr. Doolittle lounged heavily in.

"Have some gum, George?" he inquired, inserting a large piece in his own mouth.

He chewed rhythmically for a space. George waited. He knew that chewing gum was not the ultimate object of Mr. Doolittle's visit.

"Don't women beat the Dutch?" he inquired at last. "Yes sir, mister; they do!"

"What's up now?" George inquired. "The suffragists again?"

"Nope; not on the face of it they ain't. It's the Woman's Forum that's doin' this. They've got a sweet little idea. 'Seein' Whitewater Sweat' they call it.

"They're goin' around in bunches of twos, or mebbe blocks o' five, seein' all the sights; an' you know women ain't reasonable, an' you can't reason with them. They're goin' to find a pile o' things they won't like in this little burg o' ours, all right, all right. An' they'll want to have things changed right off. I want to see things changed m'self. I'd like to, but them things take time, an' that's what women won't understand.

"Jimminee, I've heard of towns all messed up and candidates ruined just because the women got wrought up over tenement-house an' fire laws an' truck like that. Yes sir, they're out seein' Whitewater this minut, or will be if you can't divert their minds. Call 'em off, George, if you can. Get 'em fussy about sumpen else."

"Why, what have I to do with it?" George inquired.

"Well, I didn't know but what you might have sumpen," said Mr. Doolittle mildly. "It's that young lady that works here, Miss Sheridan, an' your wife what's organizin' it. Planning it all out to Thorne's at lunch they was, an' Heally was sittin' at the next table and beats it to me. You can see for yerself what a hell of a mess they'll make!"

IX

BY ALICE DUER MILLER

I⊤ was a relief to both men when at this point the door of the office opened and Martin Jaffry entered.

Not since the unfortunate anti-suffrage statement of George's had Uncle Martin dropped in like this. George, looking at him with that first swift glance that often predetermines a whole interview, made up his mind that bygones were to be bygones. He greeted his uncle with the warmest cordiality.

"Well, George," said Uncle Martin, "how are things going?"

"I'm going to be elected, if that's what you mean," answered George.

Doolittle gave a snort. "Indeed, are ye?" said he. "As a friend and well-wisher, I'm sure I'm delighted to hear the news."

"Do I understand that you have your doubts, Mr. Doolittle?" Jaffry inquired mildly.

"There's two things we need and need badly, Mr. Jaffry," said Doolittle. "One's money—"

"A small campaign contribution would not be rejected?"

"But there's something we need more than money—and God knows I never expected to say them words—and that's common sense."

"Good," said Uncle Martin, "I have plenty of that, too!"

"Then for the love of Mike pass some of it on to this precious nephew of yours."

"What seems to be the matter?"

"It's them women," said Doolittle.

Uncle Martin turned inquiringly to George: "The tender flowers?" he suggested.

"Look here, Uncle Martin," said George, who had had a good

deal of this sort of thing to bear, "I don't understand you. Do you believe in woman suffrage?"

Uncle Martin contemplated a new crumpling of his long-suffering cap before he answered.

"Yes and no, George. I believe in it in the same way that I believe in old age and death. I can't avoid them by denying their existence."

"But you fight against them, and put them off as long as you can."

"But I yield a little to them, too, George. What is it? Has Genevieve become a convert to suffrage?"

"Has Genevieve—has my wife—"

Then George remembered that his uncle was an older man and that chivalry is not limited to the treatment of the weaker sex.

"No," he said with a calm hardly less magnificent than the tempest would have been, "no, Uncle Martin, Genevieve has not become a suffragist."

"Well," said Doolittle rising, as if such things were hardly worth his valuable time, "I fail to see the difference between a suffragette an' a woman who goes pokin' her nose into what—"

"You're speaking of my wife, Mr. Doolittle," said George, with a significant lighting of the eye.

"Speakin' in general," said Doolittle.

Uncle Martin was interested.

"Has Genevieve been—well, we won't say poking the nose—but taking a responsible civic interest where it would be better if she didn't?"

"It seems," answered George, casting an angry glance at his campaign manager, "that Mr. Doolittle has heard from a friend of his who overheard a conversation between Betty Sheridan and my wife at luncheon. From this he inferred that the two were planning an investigation of some of the city's problems."

Uncle Martin looked relieved.

"Oh, your wife and your stenographer. That can be stopped, I suppose, without undue exertion."

"Betty is no longer my stenographer."

"Left, has she?" said Jaffry. "I had an idea she would not stay with you long."

This intimation was not agreeable to George. He would have liked to explain that Miss Sheridan's departure had been dictated by the will of the head of the firm; in fact he opened his mouth to do so. But the remembrance that this would entail a long and wearisome exposition of his reasons caused him to remain silent, and his uncle went on:

"Well, anyhow, you can get Genevieve to drop it."

If Doolittle had not been there, George would have been glad to discuss with his uncle, who had, after all, a sort of worldly shrewdness, how far a man is justified in controlling his wife's opinions. But before an audience now a trifle unsympathetic, he could not resist the temptation of making the gesture of a man magnificently master in his own house.

He smiled quite grandly. "I think I can promise that," he said.

Doolittle got up slowly, bringing his jaws together in a relentless bite on the unresisting gum.

"Well," he said, "that's all there is to it." And he added significantly as he reached the door, "If you kin *do* it!"

When the campaign manager had gone, Uncle Martin asked very, very gently: "You don't feel any doubt of being able to do it, do you, George?"

"About my ability to control—I mean influence, my wife? I feel no doubt at all."

"And Penfield, I suppose, can tackle Betty? You won't mind my saying that of the two I think your partner has the harder job."

A slight cloud appeared upon the brow of the candidate.

"I don't feel inclined to ask any favor of Penny just at present," he said haughtily. "Has it ever struck you, Uncle Martin, that Penny has an unduly emotional, an almost feminine type of mind?"

"No," said the other, "it hasn't, but that is perhaps because I have never been sure just what the feminine type of mind is."

"You know what I mean," answered George, trying to conceal his annoyance at this sort of petty quibbling. "I mean he is too personal, over-excitable, irrational and very hard to deal with."

"Dear me," said Jaffry. "Is Genevieve like that?"

"Genevieve," replied her husband loyally, "is much better poised than most women, but—yes,—even she—all women are more or less like that."

"All women and Penny. Well, George, you have my sympathy. An excitable partner, an irrational stenographer, and a wife that's very hard to deal with!"

"I never said Genevieve was hard to deal with," George almost shouted.

"My mistake—thought you did," answered his uncle, now moving rapidly away. "Let me know the result of the interview, and we'll talk over ways and means." And he shut the door briskly behind him.

George walked to the window, with his hands in his pockets. He always liked to look out while he turned over grave questions in his mind; but this comfort was now denied to him, for he could not help being distracted by the voiceless speech still relentlessly turning its pages in the opposite window.

The heading now was:

DOES THE FIFTY-FOUR-HOUR-A-WEEK LAW APPLY TO FLOWERS?

He flung himself down on his chair with an exclamation. He knew he had to think carefully about something which he had never considered before, and that was his wife's character.

Of course he liked to think about Genevieve—of her beauty, her abilities, her charms; and particularly he liked to think about her love for him.

A week ago he would have met the present situation very simply. He would have put his arm about her and said: "My darling, I think I'd a little rather you dropped this sort of thing for the present." And that would have been enough.

But he knew it would not be enough now. He would have to have a reason, a case.

"Heavens," he thought, "imagine having to talk to one's wife as if she were the lawyer for the other side."

He did not notice that he was reproaching Genevieve for being too impersonal, too unemotional and not irrational enough.

When he went home at five, he had thought it out. He put his head into the sitting-room, where Alys was ensconced behind the tea-kettle.

"Come in, George dear," she called graciously, "and let me give you a really good cup of tea. It's some I've just ordered for you, and I think you'll find it an improvement on what you've been accustomed to."

George shut the door again, pretending he had not heard; but he had had time enough to note that dear little Eleanor was building houses out of his most treasured books.

The memory of his quarrel with his wife had been partly obliterated by memories of so many other quarrels during the day that it was only when he was actually standing in her room that he remembered how very bitter their parting had been.

He stood looking at her doubtfully, and it was she who came forward and put her arms about him. They clung to each other like two children who have been frightened by a nightmare.

"We mustn't quarrel again, George," she said. I've had a real, true, old-fashioned pain in my heart all day. But I think I understand better now than I did. I lunched with Betty and she made me see."

"What did Betty make you see?" asked George nervously, for he had not perfect confidence in Miss Sheridan's visions.

"That it was all a question of efficiency. She said that in business a man's stenographer is just an instrument to make his work easier, and if for any reason at all that instrument does not suit him he is justified in getting rid of it, and in finding one that does."

"Betty is very generous," he said coldly. He wanted to hear his wife say that she had not thought him pompous; it was very hard to be thankful for a mere ethical rehabilitation.

Part of his thought-out plan was that Genevieve must herself tell him of the Woman's Forum's investigation; it would not do for him to let her know he had heard of it through a political eavesdropper. So after a moment he added casually:

"And what else did Betty have to say?"

"Nothing much."

His heart sank. Was Genevieve becoming uncandid?

"Nothing else," he said. "Just to justify me in your eyes?"

She hesitated, "No, that was not quite all, but it is too early to talk about it yet."

"Anything that interests you, my dear, I should like to hear about from the beginning."

Perhaps Genevieve was not so unemotional after all, for at this expression of his affection, her eyes filled with tears.

"I long to tell you," she said. "I only hesitated on your account, but of course I want all your help and advice. It's this: There seems to be no doubt that the conditions under which women are working in our factories are hideous—dangerous—the law is broken with perfect impunity. I know you can't act on rumors and hearsay. Even the inspectors don't give out the truth. And so we are going to persuade the Woman's Forum to abandon its old policy of mere discussion.

"We—Betty and I—are going to get the members for once to act—to make an investigation; so that the instant you come into the office you will have complete information at your disposal—facts, and facts and facts on which you can act."

She paused and looked eagerly at her husband, who remained silent. Seeing this she went on:

"I know what you're thinking. I thought of it myself. Am I justified in using my position in the Woman's Forum to further your political career? Well, my answer is, it isn't your political career, only; it's truth and justice that will be furthered."

Here in the home there was no voiceless speech to make the view intolerable, and George moved away from his wife and walked to the window. He looked out on his own peaceful trees and lawn, and on Hanna, like a tiger in the jungle, stalking a competent little sparrow.

A temptation was assailing George. Suppose he did put his opposition to this investigation on a high and mighty ground? Suppose he announced a moral scruple? But no, he cast Satan behind him.

"Genevieve," he said, turning sharply toward her, "this question puts our whole attitude to a test. If you and I are two separate individuals, with different responsibilities, different interests, different opinions, then we ought to be consistent; that ought to mean economic independence of each other, and equal suffrage; it means that husband and wife may become business competitors and political opponents.

"But if, as you know I believe, a man and woman who love each other are one, are a unit as far as society is concerned, why then our interests are identical, and it is simply a question of which of us two is better able to deal with any particular situation."

"But that is what I believe, too, George."

"I hoped it was, dear; I know it used to be. Then you must let me act for you in this matter."

"Yes, in the end; but an investigation—"

"My darling, politics is not an ideal; it is a practical human institution. Just at present, from the political point of view, such an investigation would do me incalculable harm."

"George!"

He nodded. "It would probably lose me the election."

"But why?"

"Genevieve, am I your political representative or not?"

"You are," she smiled at him, "and my dear love as well; but may I not even know why?"

"If you dismissed the cook, and I summoned you before me and bade you give me your reasons for such an action, would you not feel in your heart that I was disputing your judgment?"

She looked at him honestly. "Yes, I should."

"And I would not do such a discourteous thing to you. In the home you are absolute. Whatever you do, whatever you decide, is right. I would not dream of questioning. Will you not give me the same confidence in my special department?"

There was a short pause; then Genevieve held out her hand.

"Yes, George," she said, "I will, but on one condition—"

"*I* did not make conditions, Genevieve."

"You do not have to, my dear. You know that I am really your representative in the house; that I am really always thinking of your wishes. You must do the same as my political representative. I mean, if I am not to do this work myself, you must do it for me."

"Even if I consider it unwise?"

"Unwise to protect women and children?"

"Genevieve," he said seriously, as one who confides something not always confided to women, "enforcing law sometimes does harm."

"But an investigation—"

"That's where you are ignorant, my dear. If an investigation is made, especially if the women mix themselves up in it, then we shall have no choice but enforcement."

She had sunk down on her sofa, but now she sprang up. "And you don't mean to enforce the law in respect of women? Is that why you don't want the investigation?"

"Not at all. You are most unjust. You are most illogical, Genevieve. All I am asking is that the whole question should not be taken up at this moment—just before election."

"But this is the only moment when we can find out whether or not you are a candidate who will do what we want."

"*We*, Genevieve! Who do you mean by 'we'?"

She stared for a second at him, her eyes growing large and dark with astonishment.

"Oh, George," she gasped finally, "I think I meant *women* when I said 'we.' George, I'm afraid I'm a *suffragist*. And oh," she added, with a sort of wail, "I don't want to be, I don't want to be!"

"Damn Betty Sheridan," exclaimed George. "This is all her doing."

His wife shook her head. "No," she said, "it wasn't Betty who made me see."

"Who was it?"

"It was you, George."

"I don't understand you."

"You made me see why women want to vote for themselves. How can you represent me, when we disagree fundamentally?"

"How can we disagree fundamentally when we love each other?"

"You mean that because we love each other, I must think as you do?"

"What else could I mean, darling?"

"You might have meant that you would think as I do."

George glanced at her in deep offense.

"We have indeed drifted far apart," he said.

At this moment there was a knock at the door, and the news was conveyed to George that Mr. Evans was downstairs asking to see him.

"Oh dear," said Genevieve, "it seems as if we never could get a moment by ourselves nowadays. What does Penny want?"

"He wants to tell me whether he intends to dissolve partnership or not."

Any fear that his wife had disassociated herself from his interests should have been dispelled by the tone in which she exclaimed: "Dissolve partnership! Penny? Well, I never in my life! Where would Penny be without you, I should like to know! He must be crazy."

These words made George feel happier than anything that had happened to him throughout this day. His self-esteem began to revive.

"I think Penny has been a little hasty," he said, judicially but not unkindly. "He lost all self-control when he heard I had let Betty go."

"Isn't that like a man," said Genevieve, "to throw away his whole future just because he loses his temper?"

George did not directly answer this question, and his wife went on. "However, it will be all right. He has seen Betty this afternoon, and she won't let him do anything foolish."

George glanced at her. "You mean that Betty will prevent his leaving the firm?"

"Of course she will."

George walked to the door.

"I seem to owe a good deal to my former stenographer," he said, "my wife, my partner; next, perhaps it will be my election."

X

BY ETHEL WATTS MUMFORD

PENNY, pacing the drawing-room with pantheresque strides, came to a tense halt as Remington entered.

"Well?" he said, his eyes hard, his unwelcoming hands thrust deep into his pockets.

That identical "well" with its uptilt of question had been on George's tongue. It was a monosyllable that demanded an answer. Penny had got ahead of him, forced him, as it were, into the witness chair, and he resented it.

"Seems to me," he began hotly, "that you were the one who was going to make the statements—'whether or no,' I believe, we were to continue in partnership."

"Perhaps," retorted Penny, with the air of allowing no great importance to that angle of the argument, "but what I want to know is, *are* you going to be a square man, and own up you were peeved into being a tyrant? And when you've done that, are you going to tell Betty, and apologize?"

George hesitated, trapped between his irritation and the still small voice.

"Look here," he said, with that amiable suavity that had won him many a concession, "you know well enough I don't want to hurt Betty's feelings. If she feels that way about it, of course I'll apologize."

His partner looked at him in blank amazement.

"Gad!" be exclaimed as if examining a particularly fine specimen of some rare beetle, "what a bounder."

"Meaning me?" snapped George.

"Don't dare to quibble. Look me in the eye."

There was a third degree fatality about the usually debonair Penny that exacted obedience. George unwillingly looked him in the eye, and had a ghastly feeling of having his suddenly realized smallness X-rayed.

"You know damned well you acted like a cad," Penny continued, "and I want to know, for all our sakes, if you're man enough to own it?"

George's fundamental honesty mastered him. Anger died from his eyes. His clenched hands relaxed and began an unconscious and nervous exploration for a cigarette.

"Since you put it that way," he said, "and it happens that my conscience agrees with you—I'll go you. I *was* a cad, and I'll tell Betty so. Confound it!" he growled, "I don't know *what's* come over me these days. I've got to get a grip on myself."

"You *bet* you have," said Penny, hauling his fists from his trousers as if with an effort. Then he grinned. "Betty said you would."

George's eyes darkened.

"And I'll tell you now," Penny went on, "since you've turned out at least half-decent, Betty'll let you off that apology thing. *She* wasn't the one who was exacting it—not she. *I* couldn't stand for your highfalutin excuses for being—well, never mind—we all get our off days. But don't you get off again like that if—"

Penny hesitated. "If you want me for a partner," which seemed the obvious conclusion, was tame. "If you want to hang on to any one's respect," he finished.

"Say, though," he murmured, "Betty'll give me 'what for' for drubbing you. She actually took your side—said—oh, never mind—tried to make me think of her just as if she was any old Mamie-the-stenog—tried to prune out personal feeling. By Jove," he ruminated, "that girl's a corker!"

He raised forgiving eyes from his contemplation of the rug.

"Well, old man, blow me to a Scotch and soda, and I'll be going. Dinged if it wouldn't have broken me all up to have busted with you, even if you are a box of prunes. Shake."

George shook, but he was far from happy. What he had gained in peace of mind he had lost in self-conceit. His resentment against the pinch of circumstance was deepening to cancerous vindictiveness.

As Pennington left with a cheery good-by and a final half-cyn-
ical word of advice "to get onto himself" George mounted the
stairs slowly and came face to face with Genevieve, obviously in
wait for him.

"What happened?" she inquired, with an anxious glance at his
corrugated brow.

George did not feel in a mood to describe his retreat, if not defeat.

"Oh, nothing. We had a highball. I think I made him—well—
it's all right."

"There, I knew Betty'd make him see reason," she smiled. "I'm
awfully glad. I've a real respect for Penny's judgment after all, you
know."

"Meaning, you have your doubts about mine."

"No, meaning only just what I said—*just* that. By the way,
George, I wish you'd take time to look into Alys' real estate. Somebody ought to, and if you're really representing her—"

"Oh, good heavens!" he exclaimed impatiently, angered by her
swift transition from his own to another's affairs. "I can't! I simply
can't! Haven't you any conception of how busy I am?"

"I know, dear; I *do* know. But something must be done. The
Health Department," she explained, "has sent in complaint after
complaint, and Miss Eliot simply won't handle the property unless
she's allowed to spend a lot setting things to rights. Alys says it's absurd; none of the other property owners out there are doing anything, and *she* won't. So, nobody's looking after it, and somebody
should."

"Who told you all this?" he demanded. "Miss E. Eliot, I suppose."

His wife nodded. "And she's right," she added.

"Well, perhaps she is," he allowed. "I'll get Allen to act as her
agent again. He's in with all the politicians; he ought to be able to
stall off the department."

The words slipped out before he realized their import, but at
Genevieve's wide stare of amazement he flushed crimson. "I
mean—lots of these complaints are really mere red tape; some self-

important employee is trying to look busy. A little investigation usually puts that straight."

"Of course," she acquiesced, and he breathed a sigh of relief.

"That happens, too, but Miss Eliot says that the conditions out there are really dreadful."

"I'll talk to Allen," said George with an affectation of easy dismissal of the subject.

But Genevieve's mind appeared to have grown suddenly persistent. At dinner she again brought up the subject, this time directing her troubled gaze and troubling words at her guest.

"Alys," she said abruptly, "I really think you ought to go out to Kentwood—to see about your property out there, I mean."

Mrs. Brewster-Smith looked up, rolling her large eyes in frank amazement.

"Go out there? What for? It isn't the sort of a district a lady cares to be seen in, I'm told; and, besides, George is looking after that for me. *He* understands such matters, and I frankly own *I* don't. Business makes me quite dizzy," she added with a flash of very white teeth.

Genevieve hesitated, then went to the point.

"But you must advise with your agent, Alys. The property is *yours.*"

Alys raised sharply penciled brows.

"I have utter confidence in George," she answered in a tone of finality that brought an adoring, look from Emelene, and her usual Boswellian echo: "*Of course.*"

George squirmed uneasily. Such a vote of confidence implied accepted responsibility, and he acknowledged to himself that he wanted to and would dodge the unwelcome burden. He turned a benign Jovian expression on Mrs. Brewster-Smith and condescended to explain.

"I have considered what is best for you, and I will myself see Allen and request him to take your real-estate affairs in charge again. Neither Sampson nor—er—Eliot is, I think, advisable for your best interests."

At the mention of the last name Genevieve's expressive face

stretched to speak; then she closed her lips with self-controlled determination. Mrs. Brewster-Smith looked at her host in scandalized amazement.

"But *I told* you," she almost whimpered, "that his wife is simply impossible."

George smiled tolerantly. "But his wife isn't doing the business. It's the business, *not* the social interests, we have to consider."

"Oh, but she *is* in the business," Alys explained. "I think it's because she's jealous of him; she wants to be around the office and watch him."

Genevieve interposed. "Mrs. Allen owns a lot of land herself, and she looks after it. It seems quite natural to me."

"But she *has* a husband," Alys rebuked.

"Yes," agreed Genevieve, "but she probably married him for a husband, not a business agent."

George felt the reins of the situation slipping from him, so he jerked the curb of conversation.

"We are beside the issue," he said in his most legal manner. "The fact is that Allen knows more about the Kentwood district and the factory values than any one else, and I feel it my duty to advise Alys to leave her affairs in his hands. I'll see him for you in the morning."

He turned to Alys with a return of tolerantly protective inflection in his voice.

Genevieve shrugged, a faint ghost of a shrug. Had George been less absorbed in his own mental discomforts, he would have discovered there and then that the matter of his speech, not the manner of his delivery, was what held his wife's attention. No longer could rounded periods and eloquent sophistry hide from her his thoughts and intentions.

A telephone call interrupted the meal. He answered it with relief, bowing a hurried, self-important excuse to the ladies. But the voice that came over the wire was not modulated in tones of flattery.

"Say," drawled the campaign manager, "you'd better get a hump on, and come over here to headquarters. There's a couple of gents here who want a word with you."

The tone was ominous, and George stiffened. "Very well, I'll be right over. But you can pretty well tell them where I stand on the main issues. Who's at headquarters?"

A snort of disgust greeted the inquiry. The snort told George that seasoned campaigners did not use the telephone with such casual lack of circumspection. The words were in like manner enlightening.

"Well, there might be Mr. Julius Cæsar, and then again Mr. George Washington might drop in. What I'm putting you wise to," he added sharply, "is that you'd better get on to your job."

There was a click as of a receiver hung up with a jerk, and a subdued giggle that testified to the innocent attention of the telephone operator.

With but a pale reflection of his usual courtesy the harassed candidate left the bosom of his family. No sooner had he taken his departure than the bosom heaved.

"My dear girl," said Alys, "if you take that tone with your husband you'll never hold him—never. Men won't stand for it. You're only hurting yourself."

"What tone?" Genevieve inquired as she rose calmly and led the way to the drawing-room.

"I mean"—Mrs. Brewster-Smith slipped a firm, white hand across Genevieve's shoulders—"you shouldn't try to force issues. It looks as if you didn't have confidence in your husband, and men, to *do* and *be* their best, must feel perfect trust from the woman they love. You don't mind my being so frank, dear, but we women must help one another—by our experience and our intuitions."

Genevieve looked at her. Oblique angles had become irritatingly fascinating. "I'm beginning to think so more and more," she replied.

"It's for your own good, dear," Alys smiled.

"Yes," Genevieve agreed. "I understand. Things that hurt are often for our good, aren't they? We have to be *made* to realize facts really to know them."

"Coffee, dear?" inquired Alys, assuming the duties of hostess.

Genevieve shook her head. "No. I find I've been rather wakeful of late: perhaps it's coffee. Excuse me. I must telephone."

A moment later she returned beaming.

"I have borrowed a car for tomorrow, and I want you and Emelene to come with me for a little spin. We ought to have a bright day; the night is wonderful. Poor George," she sighed, "I wish he didn't have to be away so much."

"His career is yours, you know," kittenishly bromidic, Emelene comforted her.

The following day fulfilled the promise of its predecessor. Clear and balmy, it invited to the outer world, and it was with pleased anticipation that Genevieve's guests prepared for the promised outing. Genevieve glanced anxiously into her gold mesh bag. The motor was hired, not borrowed.

She had permitted herself this one white lie.

She ushered her guests into the tonneau and took her place beside the chauffeur. Their first few stops were for such prosaic purchases as the household made necessary; there was a pause at the post office, another at the Forum, where Genevieve left two highly disgruntled women waiting for her while with a guilty sense of teasing her prey she prolonged her business. The sight of their stiffened figures and averted faces when she returned to them kindled a new amusement.

At last they were settled comfortably, and the car turned toward the suburbs.

The town streets were passed and lines of villa homes thinned. The ornate colonial gates of the Country Club flashed by. Now the sky to the right was dark with the smoke of the belching chimneys of many factories. For a block or two cottages of the better sort flanked the road; then, grim, ugly and dilapidated, stretched the twin "improved" sections of Kentwood and Powderville. In the air was an acrid odor. Soot begrimed everything. The sodden ground was littered with refuse between the shacks, which were dignified by the title of "Workmen's Cottages."

Amid the confusion, irregular trodden paths led, short-cutting, toward the clattering, grinding munition plants. For a space of at least half an acre around the huge iron buildings the ground, with sinister import, was kept clear of dwellings, but in all directions outside of the inclosure thousands of new yellow-pine shacks testified to the sudden demand for labor. A large weather-beaten sign-board at a wired cross-road bore the name of "Kentwood," plus the advice that the office was adjacent for the purchase or lease of the highly desirable villa sites.

The motor drew up and Genevieve alighted. For the first time since their course had been turned toward the unlovely but pro-ductive outskirts, Genevieve faced her passengers. Alys' face was pale. Emelene's expression was puzzled and worried, as a child's is worried when the child is suddenly confronted by strange and gloomy surroundings.

"There is some one in the renting office," said Genevieve with quiet determination. "I'll find out. We shall need a guide to go around with us. Emelene, you needn't get out unless you wish to."

Emelene shuffled uneasily, half rose, and collapsed helplessly back on the cushions, like a baby who has encountered the resis-tance of his buggy strap.

"I—if you'll excuse me, Genevieve, dear, I won't get out. I've only got on my thin kid slippers. I didn't expect to put foot on the pavement this morning, you know."

"Very well, then, Alys!" Genevieve's voice assumed a note of command her mild accents had never before known.

Alys' brilliant eyes snapped. "I have no desire," she said firmly, with all the dignity of an affronted lady, "to go into this matter."

"I know you haven't. But I'm going to walk through. *I* am making a report for the Woman's Forum."

Alys' face crimsoned with anger.

"You have no right to do such a thing," she exclaimed. "I shall refuse you permission. You will have to obtain a permit."

"I have one," Genevieve retorted, "from the Health Depart-ment. And—I am to meet one of the officers here."

Mrs. Brewster-Smith's descent from the tonneau was more rapid than graceful.

"What are you trying to do?" she demanded. "Genevieve, I don't understand you."

"Don't you?"

The diffident girl had suddenly assumed the incisive strength of observant womanhood.

"I think you *do*. I am going to show you your own responsibilities, if that's a possible thing. I'm not going to let you throw them on George because he's a man and your kin; and I shan't let him throw them on an irresponsible agent because he has neither the time nor the inclination to do justice to himself, to you, nor to these people to whom he is responsible."

She waved a hand down the muddy, jumbled street.

The advent of an automobile had had its effect. Eager faces appeared at windows and doors. Children frankly curious and as frankly neglected climbed over each other, hanging on the ragged fences. Two mongrel dogs strained at their chains, yelping furiously. Genevieve crossed to the little square building bearing a gilt "office" sign. There was no response to her imperative knock, but a middle-aged man appeared on the porch of the adjoining shack and observed her curiously.

"Wanta rent?" he called jeeringly.

"Are you in charge here?" Genevieve inquired.

"Sorter," he temporized. "Watcha want?"

"I want some one who knows something about it to go around Kentwood with us."

"What for?" he snarled. "I got my orders."

"From whom?" countered Genevieve.

"None of your businesses, as I can see." He eyed her narrowly. "But my orders is to keep every one nosin' around here without no good raison *out* of the place—and I don't think *you're* here to rent, nor your friend, neither. Besides, there ain't nothin' to rent."

Mrs. Brewster-Smith colored. The insult to her ownership of the premises stung her to resentment.

"My good man," she said sharply. "I happen to be the proprietor of North Kentwood."

"Then you'd better beat it." The guardian grinned. "There's a dame been here with one of them fellers from the town office."

"Where are they now?" questioned Genevieve sharply.

"Went up factory way. But if you *ain't* one of them lady nosies, you'd better beat it, I tell you."

Genevieve looked up the street. "Very well, we'll walk on up. This is North Kentwood, isn't it?"

"Ain't much choice," he shrugged, "but it is. You can smell it a mile. Say, you lady owner there"—he laughed at his own astuteness in not being taken in—"you know the monikers, don't you? South Kentwood, 'Stinktown'; North Kentwood, 'Swilltown'?" He grinned, pulled at his hip pocket and, extracting a flat glass flask, took a prolonged swig and replaced the bottle with a leer.

The two incongruous visitors were already negotiating the muddy thoroughfare between the dilapidated dwellings. Presently these gave place to roughly knocked together structures for two and three families.

The number of children was surprising. Now and again a shrill-voiced woman, who seemed the prototype of her who lived in the shoe, came to admonish her young and stare with hostile eyes at the invaders. Refuse, barrels, cans, pigs, dogs, chickens, were on all sides, with here and there a street watering trough, fed, apparently, by an occasional tap at the wide-apart hydrants, installed by the factories for protection in case of fire, as evidenced by the signs staked by the apparatus.

"What do they pay you for these cottages?" Genevieve inquired suddenly.

Mrs. Brewster-Smith, whose curiosity concerning her possessions had been aroused by the physical evidence of the same, balanced on a rut and surveyed her tormentor angrily.

"I'm sure I don't know. I've told you before I don't understand such matters, and I see nothing to be gained by coming here."

Genevieve pushed open a battered gate, walked up to the door and knocked.

"What are you doing?" her companion called, querulously.

A noise of many pattering feet on bare floors, a strident order for silence, and the door swung open. A young girl stood in the doorway. Behind her were a dozen or more children, varying from toddlers to gawky girls and boys of school age.

Genevieve's eyes widened. "Dear me," she exclaimed, "they aren't all *yours!*"

The young woman grinned mirthlessly. "I should say not!" she snapped. "They pays me to look out for 'em—their fathers and mothers in the factory. Watcha want?"

"What do you pay for a house like this?"

The hired mother's brow wrinkled, and her lips drew back in an ugly snarl.

"They robs us, these landlords does. We gotter be 'longside the works, so they robs us. What do I pay for this? Thirty a month, and at that 'tain't fit for no dawg to live in. I could knock up a shack like this with tar paper, I could.

"And what do we get? I gotter haul the water in a bucket, and cook on an oil stove, and they hists the price of the ile, 'cause he comes by in a wagon with it. The landlords is squeezing the life out of us, I tell ye."

She paused in her tirade to yell at her charges. Then she turned again to the story of her wrongs.

"And of all the pest holes I ever seen, this is the plum worst. There's chills an' fever an' typhoid till you can't rest, an' them kids is abustin' with measles an' mumps an' scarlet fever. That I ain't got 'em all myself's a miracle."

"You ought to have a district nurse and inspector," said Genevieve, amused, in spite of her indignation, at the dark picture presented.

"Distric' nothin'," the other sneered. "There ain't nothin' here but rent an' taxes—doggone if I don't quit. There's plenty to do this here mindin' work, an' I bet I could make more at the factory. They're payin' grand for overtime."

Genevieve looked at the thin shoulders and narrow chest of the girl, noted her growing pallor and wondered how long such a physique could withstand the strain of hard work and overtime. She sighed. Something of her thoughts must have shown in her face, for the girl reddened and her lips tightened. Without another word she slammed the door in her visitor's face.

Mrs. Brewster-Smith cackled thin laughter.

"That's what you get for interfering," she jeered, so angry with her hostess for this forced inspection of her source of income that she was ready to sacrifice the comforts of her extended visit to have the satisfaction of airing her resentment.

"Poor soul!" said Genevieve. "Thirty a month!" Her eyes ran over the rows of crowded shacks. "The owners must get together and *do* something here," she said. "These conditions are simply vile."

"It's probably all these people are used to," Alys snapped. "And, besides, if they went further into town it'd cost them the trolley both ways, and all the time lost. It's the location they pay for. Mr. Allen told me not two months ago he thought rents could be raised."

"If you all co-operate," Genevieve continued her own line of thought, "you could at least clean the place and make it *safe* to live in, even if they haven't any comforts."

Her face brightened. Around the corner came the strong, solid figure of Miss Eliot; behind her trotted a bespectacled young man who carried a pigskin envelope under his arm and whose expression was far from happy.

"Hello!" called Miss Eliot. "So you did come. I'm glad of it. Let me present Mr. Glass to you. The department lent him to me for the day. And what do you think of it, now that you can see it?"

"Glad to meet you," said Genevieve, nodding to the health officer. "What do I think of it? What does Mr. Glass think? That's more important. Oh, let me present you—this is Mrs. Brewster-Smith."

Miss Eliot's face showed no surprise, though her eyes twinkled, but Mr. Glass was frankly taken aback.

"Mrs. Brewster-Smith—Brewster-Smith," he stammered. "Oh—er—" he gripped his pigskin folio as if about to search its contents to verify the name. "The—er—the owner? "he inquired.

Alys stiffened. "My dear husband left me this property. I have never before seen it."

"I'm very glad," beamed Mr. Glass, "to see that we shall have your co-operation in our efforts to *do* something definite for this section—and measures must be taken quickly. As you see, there is no sanitation, no trenching, no mosquito-extermination plant. Malaria and typhoid are prevalent; it's all very bad, very bad, indeed. And you'd hardly believe, Mrs. Brewster-Smith, what difficulties we are having with the owners as a class. The five biggest have formed an association. I suppose you've heard about it. They must have made an effort to interest you"—he stopped short, remembering that her name appeared on the lists of the "Protective League."

"Really"—Alys had recovered her hauteur and the aloofness becoming the situation—"I know nothing whatever about what measures my agents have thought it advisable to take."

Mr. Glass choked and glanced uneasily at Miss Eliot.

That lady grinned, almost the grin of a gamin. "You needn't look at *me*, Mr. Glass. I don't represent Mrs. Brewster-Smith."

"Oh, I know, I know," Mr. Glass hastened to exonerate his companion.

"I believe Miss Eliot declined the honor," Genevieve's voice was heard.

"I did," the agent affirmed. She laughed shortly. "Otherwise you would hardly find me here in my present capacity. One does not 'run with the hare and hunt with the hounds,' you know."

Alys lost her temper. It seemed to her she was ruthlessly being forced to shoulder responsibilities she had been taught to shirk as a sacred feminine right. Therefore, feeling injured, she voiced her innocence.

"Your husband, my dear Genevieve, has been good enough to administer my little estate. Whatever he has done, or now plans to do, meets with *my* entire approval."

The thrust went home in more directions than one. Miss Eliot turned her frank gaze upon the speaker, while she slowly nodded her head as if studying a perfect specimen of a noxious species. Mr. Glass gasped. There was political material in the statement. He looked anxiously at the wife of the gentleman implicated, but in her was no fear and no manner of trembling. Instead, the light of battle shone in her eyes.

"My dear Alys," she said, "my husband has told you that he is too busy a man to give your affairs his personal attention. He can only advise you and turn the executive side over to another. His experience does not extend to the stock market or to real estate. It is an imposition to throw your burdens upon him. If you derive benefits from ownership, you must educate yourself to accept your duty to society."

"Indeed!" flared Alys, furious at this public arraignment. "May I ask if you intend to continue this insulting attitude?"

"If you mean, do I expect hereafter to be a live woman and not a parasite—I do."

Mrs. Brewster-Smith turned on her heel and walked away, teetering over the ruts and holes of the path.

Genevieve looked distressed. "I'm sorry," she breathed, "I'm ashamed, but it *had* to come out. I—I couldn't stand it any longer. I—beg everybody's pardon. I'm sure, it was awfully bad manners of me. Oh, dear—" she faltered, half turned, and, with a gesture of appeal toward Mrs. Brewster-Smith's slowly retreating back, moved as if to follow.

"I wouldn't go after her," said E. Eliot. "Of course, you haven't had experience. You don't know how much self-restraint you've got to build up, but you're here now, and I'm sure Mr. Glass understands. *He's* got to come up against all sorts of exasperations on *his* job, too. He won't take any stock in Mrs. Brewster-Smith's trying to tie your husband up to these wretched conditions.

"He's looking forward to seeing an honest, public-spirited district attorney get into office—even if your husband doesn't yet see that women have anything to say about it. They may heckle him in order to force him to come out on his intentions about the graft, and the eight-hour day, and the enforcement of the law, but they don't doubt his honesty. When he know's what's what, I guess the public can trust him to do the right thing. Only, he's got to be shown."

As she talked, giving Genevieve time to recover from her upheaval, the three investigators were plowing their way up and down byways equally depressing and insanitary. Silence ensued. Occasionally an expression of commiseration or condemnation escaped one or another of the party.

Suddenly a raucous whistle tore the air, followed by another and another, declaring the armistice of the noon hour. Iron gates in the surrounding wall were opened, a stream of men and women poured out, grimed, sweat-streaked and voluble. The two women and their escort paused and watched the oncoming swarm of humanity.

Around the corner, just ahead, strode a giant of a man, followed by a red-faced, unkempt, familiar figure—the man in charge of the renting office. The giant came forward threateningly.

"What youse doing?" he growled. He jerked his jersey, displaying a brass badge, P. A. Guard.

"Git outer here—git," he called.

Mr. Glass stepped forward, displaying his Health Department permit. The giant laughed.

"Say, sonny," he sneered, "that don't go—see. Them tin fakes don't git by. If you're one of them guys, you come here wit' McLaughlin, and youse can rubber. But we've had enough of this stuff. Them dames is no blind, neither. I'm guard for the owners here, and we ain't takin' no chances wit' trouble makers—git. Git a move on!"

"The department," spluttered Glass, "shall hear of this."

"That's all right. McLaughlin's the boss. Tell 'em not to send a kid to do a man's job."

Genevieve was too amazed to protest. It was her first experience of defiance of Law and Order by Law and Order.

Meanwhile, the first stragglers of the released army of toilers were nearly upon them. The giant observed their approach, and the look of menace deepened on his huge, congested face.

"Move on, now—move on," be snarled, and herded them forward in advance of the workers.

Sheepishly the three obeyed, but Miss Eliot was not silent.

"Your name?" she demanded in judicial command.

The very terseness of her question seemed to jerk an unwilling answer from the guard.

"Michael Mehan."

"And you're employed by the Owners' Protective League?"

"Sure."

"Have they given you orders to keep strangers out of the district?"

"I have me orders, and I know what they be. I'm duly sworn in as extra guard—and I'm not the only one, neither."

"Did *he* come after you?" Miss Eliot indicated the ruffian at his side.

"I seen the lady owner blew the bunch," that worthy remarked with a hoarse chuckle. "I wised Mike, all right. Whatcha goin' to do about it?"

"Mrs. Brewster-Smith, the owner," Miss Eliot observed, "didn't seem to know that she had employed you. How about that?"

"I'm put here by the O. P. L. That's good enough fer yer lady owner—not—ain't it? The things them nosey dames thinks they can git by wit'!" he observed to the guard, and swore an oath that made Mr. Glass turn to him with unexpected fury.

"You may pretend to think that I'm not what I represent myself to be, but let me tell you, McLaughlin is going to hear of this. One more insult to these ladies and I'll make it my business to go personally to your employers. Get me?"

"Shut your trap, Jim," snarled Mehan. "Yer ain't got no orders fer no fancy language." He leered at Genevieve. "Now we've shooed the chickens out, we're tru'." With a wave of his huge paw he indicated the highway the turn of the path revealed.

Genevieve looked to the right, where the car should be waiting her. It was gone. Evidently the indignant Mrs. Brewster-Smith had expedited the departure. Miss Eliot read her discomfiture.

"My car is right down here behind that palatial mansion with the hole in the roof and the tin-can extension. Thank you very much for your escort," she added, turning to the two representatives of the Protective League. "My name, by the way, is E. Eliot. I am a real-estate agent and my office is at 22 Braston Street. You might mention it in your report."

The little car stood waiting, surrounded by a group of admiring children. Its owner stepped in briskly, backed around and received her passengers.

"Well," she smiled as they drew out on the traveled highway, "how do you like the purlieus of our noble little city?"

Genevieve was silent. Then she spoke with conviction.

"When George is in power—and he's *got* to be—the Law will be the Law. I know him."

XI

BY MARJORIE BENTON COOKE

GEORGE REMINGTON walked toward headquarters with more assurance than he felt. He resented Doolittle's command that he appear at once. He was beginning to realize the pressure which these campaign managers were bringing to bear upon him. He was not sure yet how far he could go, in out-and-out defiance of them and their dictates.

He knew that he had absolutely no ambitions, no interests in common with these schemers, whose sole idea lay in party patronage, in manipulating every political opportunity—in short, in reaping where they had sown. The question now confronting him was this: was he prepared to sell his political birthright for the mess of pottage they offered him?

He stood a second at the door of the office, peering through the reeking, smoke-filled atmosphere, to get a bird's-eye view of the situation before he entered.

Mr. Doolittle sat on the edge of a table monologuing to Wes' Norton and Pat Noonan. Mr. Norton was the president of the Whitewater Commercial Club, composed of the leading merchants of the town, and Mr. Noonan was the apostle of the liquor interests. Remington felt his back stiffen as he stepped among them.

"Good-evening, gentlemen," he said briskly.

"H'are ye, George?" drawled Doolittle.

"There was something you wanted to discuss with me?"

"I dunno as there's anything to discuss, but there's a few things Wes' an' Pat an' me'd like to say to ye. There ain't no two ways of thinkin' about the prosperity of Whitewater, ye know, George. The merchants in this town is satisfied with the way things is boomin'. The factory workers is gittin' theirs, with high wages an' overtime.

The stockholders is makin' no kick on the dividends—as ye know, George, being one of them.

"Now, we don't want nuthin' to disturb all this. If the fact'ries is crackin' the law a bit, why, it ain't the first time such things has got by the inspector. The fact'ry managers 'd like some assurance from ye that ye're goin' to keep yer hands off before they line up the fact'ry hands to vote for ye."

Doolittle paused here. George nodded.

"When are ye comin' out with a plain statement of yer intentions, George?" inquired Mr. Norton in a conciliatory tone.

"The voters in this town will get a clear statement of my stand on all the issues of this campaign in plenty of time, gentlemen."

"That's all right fer the voter, but ye can't stall *us* wit' that kind of talk—" began Noonan.

"Wait a minute, Pat," counseled Doolittle. "George means all right. He's new to this game, but he means to stand fer the intrusts of his party, don't ye, George?"

"I should scarcely be the candidate of that party if I did not."

"I ain't interested in no oratory. Are ye or are ye not goin' to keep yer hands off the prosperity of Whitewater?" demanded Noonan angrily.

"Look here, Noonan, I am the candidate for this office—you're not. I intend to do as my conscience dictates. I will not be hampered at every turn, nor told what to say and what to think. I must get to these things in my own way."

"Don't ye fergit that ye're *our* candidate, that ye are to express the opinion of the people who will elect ye, and not any dam' theories of yer own—"

"I think I get your meaning, Noonan."

George spoke with a smile which for some reason disconcerted Noonan. He sensed with considerable irritation the social and class breach between himself and Remington, and while he did not understand it he resented it. He called him "slick" to Wes' and Doolittle and loudly bewailed their choice of him as candidate.

"Then there's that P. L. bizness, Pat—don't fergit that," urged Wes'.

"I ain't fergittin' it. There's too much nosin' round Kentwood

district by the women, George. Too much talkin'. Ye'd better call
that off right now. Property owners down there is satisfied, an' they
got *their* rights, ye know."

"I suppose you know what the conditions down there are?"

"Sure we know, George, and we want to clean it up down
there just as much as you do," said the pacific Doolittle; "but what
we're sayin' is, this ain't the time to do it. Later, mebbe, when the
conditions is jest right—"

"Somebody has got the women stirred up fer fair. It's up to
you to call 'em off, George," said Mr. Norton.

"How can I call them off?"—tartly.

"Ye can put the brakes on Mrs. Remington and that there
Sheridan girl, can't ye?"

"Miss Sheridan is no longer in my employ. As for Mrs. Remington, if she is not one in spirit with me, I cannot force her to be.
Every human being has a right to—"

"Some change sence ye last expressed yerself, George. Seems
like I recall ye sayin', 'I'll settle that!' " remarked Doolittle coldly.

"We will leave my wife's name out of the discussion, please,"
said George with tardy but noble loyalty.

"Well, them two I mentioned can stir up some trouble; but
they ain't the brains of their gang, by a long shot. It's this E. Eliot
we gotta deal with. She's as smart, if not smarter, than any man in
this town. She's smarter than you, George—or me, either," he
added consolingly.

"I've seen her about, but I've never talked to her. What sort of
woman is she?"

"Quiet, sensible kind. Ye keep thinking, 'How reasonable that
woman is,' till ye wake up and find she's got ye hooked on one of
the horns of yer own damfoolishness! Slick as they make 'em and
straight as a string—that's E. Eliot."

"What do you want me to do about it?"—impatiently.

"Are ye aimin' to answer them voiceless questions?" Pat inquired.

Silence.

"Plannin' to tear down Kentwood and enforce them factory
laws?" demanded Wes' Norton.

Still no answer.

"I'm jest callin' yer attention to the fact that this election is gittin' nearer every day."

"What am I to do with her? I can't afford to show we're afraid of her."

"Huh."

"I can't bribe her to stop."

"I'd like to see the fella that would try to bribe E. Eliot," Doolittle chuckled. "Wouldn't be enough of him left to put in a teacup."

"Then we've got to ignore her."

"*We* can ignore her, all right, George; but the women an' some of the voters ain't ignoring her. It's my idea she's got a last card up her sleeve to play the day before we go to the polls that'll fix us."

"Have you any plan in your mind?"

Doolittle scratched his head, wrestling with thought.

"We was thinking that if she could be called away suddenly, and detained till after election—" he began meaningly.

"You mean—"

"Something like that."

"I won't have it, not if I lose the election. I won't stoop to kidnapping a woman like a highwayman. What do you take me for, Doolittle?"

"Georgie, politics ain't no kid-glove bizness. It ain't what *you* want; you're jest a small part of this affair. You're *our* candidate, and we *got* to win this here election. Do you get me?"

He shot out his underjaw, and there was no sign of his usual good humor.

"Well, but—"

"You don't have to know anything about this. We'll handle it. You'll be pertected to the limit; don't you worry," sneered Noonan.

"But you can't get away with this old-fashioned stuff nowadays, Doolittle," protested Remington.

"Can't we? You jest leave it to your Uncle Benjamin. You don't know nothing about this. See?"

"I know it's a dirty, low, underhanded—"

"George," remarked Mr. Doolittle, slowly hoisting his big body on to its short legs, "in politics we don't call a spade a spade. We call it 'a agricultural implument.'"

With this sage remark Mr. Doolittle took his departure, followed by the other prominent citizens.

George sat where they left him, head in hands, for several moments. Then he sprang up and rushed to the door to call them back.

He would not stand it—he would not win at that price. He had conceded everything they had demanded of him up to this point, but here he drew the line. Ever since that one independent fling of his about suffrage they had treated him like a naughty child. What did they think he was—a rubber doll? He would telephone Doolittle that he would rather give up his candidacy. Here he paused.

Suppose he did withdraw, nobody would understand. The town would think the women had frightened him off. He couldn't come out now and denounce the machine methods of his party. Every eye in Whitewater was focused on him; his friends were working for him; the district attorneyship was the next step in his career; Genevieve expected him to win—no, he must go through with it! But after he got into office, then he would show them! He would take orders from no one. He sat down again and moodily surveyed the future.

In the days which followed, another mental struggle was taking place in the Remington family.

Poor Genevieve was like a woman struck by lightning. She felt that her whole structure of life had crashed about her ears. In one blinding flash she had seen and condemned George because he considered political expediency. She realized that she must think for herself now and not rely on him for the family celebration. She had conceived her whole duty in life to consist in being George's wife; but now, by a series of accidents, she had become aware of the great social responsibilities, the larger human issues, which men and women must meet together.

Betty and E. Eliot had pointed out to her that she knew nothing of the conditions in her own town. They assured her that it was as much her duty to know about such things as to know the condition of her own back yard.

Then came the awful revelations of Kentwood—human beings huddled like rats; children swarming, dirty and hungry! She could not bear to remember the scenes she had witnessed in Kentwood.

She recalled the shock of Alys Brewster-Smith's indifference to all that misery! The widow's one instinct had seemed to be to fight E. Eliot and the health officer for their interference. Stranger still, the tenants did not want to be moved out, driven on. The whole situation was confused, but in it at least one thing stood out clearly: Genevieve realized, during the sleepless night after her visit to Kentwood, that she hated Cousin Alys!

The following Sunday, when she put on her coat, she found a souvenir of that visit in her pocket, a soiled reminder of poverty and toil. She remembered picking it up and noting that it was the factory pass of one Marya Slavonsky. She had intended to leave it with some one in the district, but evidently in the excitement of her enforced exit she had thrust it into her pocket.

This Marya worked in the factories. She was one of that grimy army Genevieve had seen coming out of the factory gate, and she went home to that pen which Cousin Alys provided. Marya was a girl of Genevieve's own age, perhaps, while she, Genevieve, had this comfortable home, and George! She had been blind, selfish, but she would make up for it, she *would!*

She would make a study of the needs of such people; she would go among them like St. Agatha, scattering alms and wisdom. George might have his work; she had found hers! She would begin with the factory girls. She would waken them to what had so lately dawned on her. How could she manage it? The rules of admission in the munition factories were very strict.

Then again her eye fell upon the soiled card and a great idea was born in her brain. Dressed as a factory girl, she would use Marya's card to get her into the circle of these new-found sisters. She would see how and where they worked. She would report it all to the Forum and to George. She could be of use to George at last.

She remembered Betty's statement that at midnight in the factories the women and girls had an hour off. That was the time she chose, with true dramatic instinct.

She rummaged in the attic for an hour, getting her costume ready. She decided on an old black suit and a shawl which had belonged to her mother. She carried these garments to her bedroom and hid them there. Then, with Machiavellian finesse, she laid her plans.

She would slip out of bed at half-past eleven o'clock, taking care not to waken George, and she would dress and leave the house by the side door. By walking fast she could reach by midnight the factory to which she had admission.

It annoyed her considerably to have George announce at luncheon that he had a political dinner on for the evening and probably would not be home before midnight. He grumbled a little over the dinner. "The campaign," he said, "really ended yesterday. But Doolittle thought it was wise to have a last round-up of the business men, and give them a final speech."

Genevieve acquiesced with a sympathetic murmur, but she was disappointed. Merely to walk calmly out of the house at eleven o'clock lessened the excitement. However, she decided upon leaving George a note explaining that she had gone to spend the night with Betty Sheridan.

She looked forward to the long afternoon with impatience. Cousin Emelene was taking her nap. Mrs. Brewster-Smith left immediately after lunch to make a call on one of her few women friends. Genevieve tried to get Betty on the telephone, but she was not at home.

It was with a thrill of pleasure that she saw E. Eliot coming up the walk to the door. She hurried downstairs just as the maid explained that Mrs. Brewster-Smith was not at home.

"Oh, won't you come in and see me for a moment, Miss Eliot?" Genevieve begged. "I do so want to talk to you."

E. Eliot hesitated. "The truth is, I am fearfully busy today, even though it's Sunday. I wanted to get five minutes with Mrs. Brewster-Smith about those cottages—" she began.

Genevieve laid a detaining hand on her arm and led her into the living-room.

"She's hopeless! I can hardly bear to have her in my house after the way she acted about those fearful places."

"Well, all that district is the limit, of course. She isn't the only landlord."

"But she didn't *see* those people."

"She's human, I guess—didn't want to see disturbing things."

"I would have torn down those cottages with my own hands!" burst forth Genevieve.

E. Eliot stared. "No one likes her income cut down, you know," she palliated.

"Income! What is that to human decencies?" cried the newly awakened apostle.

"Your husband doesn't entirely agree with you in some of these matters, I suppose."

"Oh, yes he does, in his heart! But there's something about politics that won't let you come right out and say what you think."

"Not after you've come right out once and said the wrong thing," laughed E. Eliot. "I'm afraid you will have to use your indirect influence on him, Mrs. Remington."

Genevieve threw her cards on the table.

"Miss Eliot, I am just beginning to see how much there is for women to do in the world. I want to do something big—the sort of thing you and Betty Sheridan are doing—to rouse women. What can I do?"

E. Eliot scrutinized the ardent young face with amiable amusement.

"You can't very well help us just now without hurting your husband's chances and embarrassing him in the bargain. You see, we're trying to embarrass him. We want him to kick over the traces and tell what he's going to do as district attorney of this town."

"But can't I do something that won't interfere with George? Couldn't I investigate the factories, or organize the working girls?"

"My child, have you ever organized anything?" exclaimed E. Eliot.

"No."

"Well, don't begin on the noble working girl. She doesn't organize easily. Wait until the election is over. Then you come in on our schemes and we'll teach you how to do things. But don't butt in now, I beg of you. Misguided, well-meaning enthusiasts like you can do more harm to our cause than all the anti-suffragists in this world!"

With her genial, disarming smile, E. Eliot rose and departed. She chuckled all the way back to her rooms over the idea of Remington's bride wanting to take the field with the enemies of her wedded lord.

"Women, women! God bless us, but we're funny!" mused E. Eliot.

Genevieve liked her caller immensely, and she thought over her advice, but she determined to let it make no difference in her plans.

She saw her work cut out for her. She would not flinch!

She would do her bit in the great cause of women—no, of humanity. The flame of her purpose burned steadily and high.

At a quarter-past eleven that night a slight, blackclad figure, with a shawl over its head, softly closed the side door of the Remington house and hurried down the street. Never before had Genevieve been alone on the streets after dark. She had not foreseen how frightened she would be at the long, dark stretches, nor how much more frightened when any one passed her. Two men spoke to her. She sped on, turning now this way, now that, without regard to direction—her eyes over her shoulder, in terror lest she be followed.

So it was that she plunged around a corner and into the very arms of E. Eliot, who was sauntering home from a political meeting, where she had been a much-advertised speaker. She was in the habit of prowling about by herself. Tonight she was, as usual, unattended—unless one observed two burly workingmen who walked slowly in her wake.

"Oh, I beg your pardon," came a gently modulated voice from behind the shawl. E. Eliot stared.

"No harm done here. Did I hurt you?" she replied.

She thought she heard an involuntary "Oh!" from beneath the shawl.

"No, thanks. Could you tell me how to get to the Whitewater Arms and Munitions Factory? I'm all turned around."

"Certainly. Two blocks that way to the State Road, and half a mile north on that. Shall I walk to the road with you?"

"Oh, no, thank you," the girl answered and hurried on.

E. Eliot stood and watched her. Where had she heard that voice? She knew a good many girls who worked at the factories, but none of them spoke like that. All at once a memory came to her: "Couldn't I investigate something, or organize the working girls?" Mrs. George Remington!

"The little fool," ejaculated the other woman, and turned promptly to follow the flying figure.

The two burly gentlemen in the rear also turned and followed, but E. Eliot was too busy planning how to manage Mrs. Remington to notice them. She had to walk rapidly to keep her quarry in sight. As she came within some thirty yards of the gate she saw Genevieve challenge the gatekeeper, present her card and slip inside, the gate clanging to behind her.

E. Eliot broke into a jog trot, rounded the corner of the wall, pulled herself up quickly, using the stones of the wall as footholds. She hung from the top and let herself drop softly inside, standing perfectly still in the shadow. At the same moment the two burly gentlemen ran round the corner and saw nothing.

"I told ye to run—" began one of them fiercely.

"Aw, shut up. If she went over here, she'll come out here. We'll wait."

The midnight gong and the noise of the women shuffling out into the courtyard drowned that conversation for E. Eliot. She stood and watched the gatekeeper saunter indoors, not waiting for the man who relieved him on duty. She watched Genevieve go forward and meet the factory hands.

The newcomer shyly spoke to the first group. The eavesdropper could not hear what she said. But the crowd gathered about the speaker, shuffling, chaffing, finally listening. Somebody captured the gatekeeper's stool and Genevieve stood on it.

"What I want to tell you is how beautiful it is for women to stand together and work together to make the world better," she began.

"Say, what is your job?" demanded a girl, suspicious of the soft voice and modulated speech.

"Well, I—I only keep house now. But I intend to begin to do a great deal for the community, for all of you—"

"She keeps house—poor little overworked thing!"

"But the point is, not what you do, but the spirit you do it in—"

"What is this, a revival meetin'?"

"So I want to tell you what the women of this town mean to do."

"Hear! Hear! Listen at the suffragette!"

"First, we mean to clean up the Kentwood district. You all know how awful those cottages are."

"Sure; we live in 'em!"

"We intend to force the landlords to tear them down and improve all that district."

"Much obliged, lady, and where do we go?" demanded one of her listeners.

"You must have better living conditions."

"But where? Rents in this town has boomed since the war began. Ain't that got to you yet? There ain't no place left fer the poor."

"Then we must find places and make them healthy and beautiful."

"For the love of Mike! She's talkin' about heaven, ain't she?"

"She's talkin' through her hat!" cried another.

"Then, we mean to make the factories obey the laws. They have no right to make you girls work here at night."

"Who's makin' us?"

"We are going to force the factories to obey the letter of the law on our statute books."

A thin, flushed girl stepped out of the crowd and faced her.

"Say, who is 'we'?"

"Why, all of us, the women of Whitewater."

"How are we goin' to repay the women of Whitewater fer tearin' down our homes an' takin' away our jobs? Ain't there somethin' we can do to show our gratitood?" the new speaker asked earnestly.

"Go to it—let her have it, Mamie Flynn!" cried the crowd.

"Oh, but you mustn't look at it that way! We must all make some sacrifices—"

"Cut that slush! What do you know about sacrifices? I'm on to you. You're one of them uptown reformers. What do you know about sacrifices? Ye got a sure place to sleep, ain't ye? Ye've got a full belly an' a husband to give ye spendin' money, ain't ye? Don't ye come down here gittin' our jobs away an' then fergettin' all about us!"

There was a buzz of agreement and an undertone of anger which to an experienced speaker would have been ominous. But Genevieve blundered on: "We only want to help you—"

"We don't want yer help ner yer advice. You keep yer hands off our business! Do yer preachin' uptown—that's where they need it. Ask the landlords of Kentwood and the stockholders in the munition factories to make some sacrifices, an' see where that gits ye! But don't ye come down here, a-spyin' on us, ye dirty—"

The last words were happily lost as the crowd of girls closed in on Genevieve with cries of "Spy!" "Scab!" "Throw her out!"

They had nearly torn her clothes off before E. Eliot was among them. She sprang up on the chair and shouted:

"Girls—here, hold on a minute."

There was a hush. Some one called out: "It's Miss E. Eliot."

"Listen a minute. Don't waste your time getting mad at this girl. She's a friend of mine. And you may not believe me, but she means all right."

"What's she pussyfootin' in here for?"

"Don't you know the story of the man from Pittsburgh who died and went on?" cried E. Eliot. "Some kindly spirit showed him round the place, and the newcomer said: 'Well, I don't think heaven's got anything on Pittsburgh.' 'This isn't heaven!' said the spirit."

There was a second's pause, and then the laugh came.

"Now, this girl has just waked up to the fact that Whitewater isn't heaven, and she thought you'd like to hear the news! I'll take the poor lamb home, put cracked ice on her head and let her sleep it off."

They laughed again.

"Go to it," said the erstwhile spokeswoman for the working girls.

E. Eliot called them a cheery good-night. The factory girls drifted away, in little groups, leaving Genevieve, bedraggled and hysterical, clinging to her rescuer.

"They would have killed me if you hadn't come!" she gasped.

E. Eliot thought quickly.

"Stand here in the shadow of the fence till I come back," she said. "It will be all right. I've got to run into the office and send a telephone message. I have a pal there who will let me do it."

"You—you won't be long?"

It was clear that the nerve of Mrs. Remington was quite gone.

"I won't be gone five minutes."

E. Eliot was as good as her word.

When she returned she seized the stool on which her companion had made her maiden speech—ran to the wall, placed it at the spot where she had made her entrance and urged Genevieve to climb up and drop over; as she obeyed, E. Eliot mounted beside her. They dropped off, almost at the same moment—into arms upheld to catch them.

Genevieve screamed, and was promptly choked.

"What'll we do with this extra one?" asked a hoarse voice.

"Bring her. There's no time to waste now. If ye yell again, ye'll both be strangled," the second speaker added as he led the way toward the road, where the dimmed lights of a motor car shone.

He was carrying E. Eliot as if she were a doll. Behind him his assistant stumbled along, bearing, less easily but no less firmly, the wife of the candidate for district attorney!

XII

BY WILLIAM ALLEN WHITE

As the two gagged women—one comfortably gagged with more or less pleasant bandages made and provided, the other gagged by the large, smelly hand of an entire stranger to Mrs. George Remington—whom she was trying impolitely to bite, by way of introduction—were speeding through the night, Mr. George Remington, ending a long and late speech before the Whitewater Business Men's Club, was saying these things:

"I especially deplore this modern tendency to talk as though there were two kinds of people in this country—those interested in good government, and those interested in bad government. We are all good Americans. We are all interested in good government. Some of us believe good government may be achieved through a protective tariff and a proper consideration for prosperity [cheers], and others, in their blindness, bow down to wood and stone!"

He smiled amiably at the laughter, and continued:

"But while some of us see things differently as to means, our aims are essentially the same. You don't divide people according to trades and callings. I deplore this attempt to set the patriotic merchant against the patriotic saloonkeeper; the patriotic follower of the race track against the patriotic manufacturer.

"Here is my good friend, Benjie Doolittle. When he played the ponies in the old days, before he went into the undertaking and furniture business, was he less patriotic than now? Was he less patriotic then than my Uncle Martin Jaffry is now, with all his manufacturer's interest in a stable government? And is my Uncle Martin Jaffry more patriotic than Pat Noonan? Or is Pat less patriotic than our substantial merchant, Wesley Norton?

"Down with this talk that would make lines of moral and patriotic cleavage along lines of vocation or calling. I want no votes of those who pretend that the good Americans should vote in one box and the bad Americans in another box. I want the votes of those of all castes and cults who believe in prosperity [loud cheers], and I want the votes of those who believe in the glorious traditions of our party, its magnificent principles, its martyred heroes, its deathless name in our history!"

It was, of course, an after-dinner speech. Being the last speech of the campaign it was also a highly important one. But George Remington felt, as he sat listening to the din of the applause, that he had answered rather neatly those who said he was wabbling on the local economic issue and was swaying in the wind of socialist agitation which the women had started in Whitewater.

As he left the hotel where the dinner had been given, he met his partner on the sidewalk.

"Get in, Penny," he urged, jumping into his car.

"Come out to the house for the night, and we'll have Betty over to breakfast. Then she and Genevieve and you and I will see if we can't restore the *ante-bellum modus vivendi!* Come on! Emelene and Alys always breakfast in bed, anyway, and it will be no trouble to get Betty over."

The two men rode home in complacent silence. It was long past midnight. They sat on the veranda to finish their cigars before going into the house.

"Penny," asked George suddenly, "what has Pat Noonan got in this game—I mean against the agitation by the women and this investigation of conditions in Kentwood? Why should he agonize over it?

"Is he fussing about it?"

"Is he? Do you think I'd tie his name up in a public speech with Martin Jaffry if Pat wasn't off the reservation? You could see him swell up like a pizened pup when I did it! I hope Uncle Martin will not be offended."

"He's a good sport, George. But say—what did Pat do to give you this hunch?"

Remington smoked in meditative silence, then answered:

"Well, Penny, I had to raise the devil of a row the other day to keep Pat from ribbing up Benjie Doolittle and the organization to a frame-up to kidnap this Eliot person."

"Kidnap E. Eliot!" gasped the amazed Evans.

"Kidnap that very pest. And I tell you, man, if I hadn't roared like a stuck ox they would have done it! Fancy introducing 'Prisoner of Zenda' stuff into the campaign in Whitewater! Though I will say this, Penny, as between old army friends and college chums," continued Mr. Remington earnestly, "if a warrior bold with spurs of gold, who was slightly near-sighted and not particular about his love being so damned young and fair, would swoop down and carry this E. Eliot off to his princely donjon, and would let down the portcullis for two days, until the election is over, it would help some! Though otherwise I don't wish her any bad luck!"

The old army friend and college chum laughed.

"Well, that's your end of the story! I'm mighty glad you stopped it. Here's my end. You remember two-fingered Moll, who was our first client? The one who insisted on being referred to as a lady? The one who got converted and quit the game and who thought she was being pursued by the racetrack gang because she was trying to live decent?"

George smiled in remembrance.

"Well, she called me up to know if there was any penalty for renting a house to Mike the Goat and his wife and old Salubrious the Armenian, who had a lady friend they were keeping from the cops against her will. She said they weren't going to hurt the lady, and I could see her every day to prove it. I advised her to keep out of it, of course; but she was strong for it, because of what she called the big money. I explained carefully that if anything should happen, her past reputation would go against her. But she kept saying it was straight, until I absolutely forbade her to do it, and she promised not to."

"Mike and his woman, and Old Salubrious!" echoed Remington. "And E. Eliot locked up with them for two days!"

He shivered, partly at the memory of his own mealy-mouthed protest.

"Well," he said, and there was an air of finality in his tone, "I'm glad I stopped the whole infamous business."

Mentally he decided to get Noonan on the telephone the first thing in the morning and make certain that the plan was abandoned. He continued his chat with Evans.

"But, Penny, why this agonizing of Noonan? What has he to lose by the better conditions in Kentwood? Why should he—"

Outside of a neat white dwelling in the suburbs of Whitewater, four figures were struggling in the night toward a vine-covered door—that door which appeared so attractively in the *Welfare Bulletin* of the Toledo Blade Steel Company's publicity program as the "prize garden home of J. Agricola, roller."

A woman stood in the doorway, holding the door open. Two women, who had been carried by two men, from an automobile at the gate, were forced through. There the men left them with their hostess.

"I was only looking for one of yez," she said, hospitably, "but you're bote welcome. Now, ladies I'm goin' to make you comfortable. It won't do no good to scream, so I'm goin' to take your gags off. And I hope you, lady, haven't been inconvenienced by a handkerchief. We could just as well have arranged for your comfort, too."

"Madam," gasped E. Eliot, who was the first to be released to speech, "it is unimportant who I am. But do you know that this woman with me is Mrs. George Remington, the wife of the candidate for district attorney—Mr. George Remington of Whitewater? There has been a mistake."

The hostess looked at Genevieve, who nodded a tearful confirmation. But the woman only smiled.

"My man don't make mistakes," she said laconically. "And, what's more to the point, miss, he's a friend of George Remington, and why should he be giving his lady a vacation? You are E. Eliot, and your friends think you're workin' too hard, so they're goin' to give you a nice rest. Nothin' will happen to you if you are a lady, as I think you are. And when I find out who this other lady is, we'll make her as welcome as you!"

She went out of the room, locking the door behind her as the two women struggled vainly with their bonds. In an instant she returned.

"My man says to tell the one who thinks she's Mrs. George Remington that she's spendin' the week-end with Mrs. Napoleon Boneypart," she called. "My man says he's a good friend of George Remington and is supportin' him for district attorney, and that's how he can make it so pleasant here.

"And I'll tell you something else," she continued proudly. "When George got married, it was my man that went up and down Smoky Row and seen all the girls and got 'em to give a dollar apiece for them lovely roses labeled 'The Young Men's Republican Club.' Mr. Doolittle he seen to that. My man really collected fifty dollars more'n he turned in, and I got a diamond-set wrist watch with it! So, you see, we're real friendly with them Remingtons, and we're glad to see you, Mrs. Remington!"

"Oh, how horrible!" cried Genevieve. "There were eight dozen of those roses from the Young Men's Republican Club, and to think—Oh, to think—"

"Well, now, George," cried Mr. Penfield Evans, "just stop and think. Use your bean, my boy! What is the one thing on earth that puts the fear of God into Pat Noonan? It's prohibition. Look at the prohibition map out West and at the suffrage map out West. They fit each other like the paper on the wall. Whatever women may lack in intelligence about some things, there is one thing woman knows—high and low, rich and poor! She knows that the saloon is her enemy, and she hits it; and Pat Noonan, seeing this rise of women investigating industry, makes common cause with Martin Jaffry and the whole employing class of Whitewater against the nosey interference of women.

"And Pat Noonan is depending on you," continued Evans. "He expects you to rise. He expects you to go to Congress—possibly to the Senate, and he figures that he wants to be dead sure you'll not get to truckling to decency on the liquor question. So he ties you up—or tries you out for a tie-up or a kidnapping; and Benjie Doolittle, who likes a sporting event, takes a chance that you'll stand hitched in a plan to rid the community of a political pest without seriously hurting the pest—a friendless old maid who won't be missed for a day or two, and whose disappearance can be hushed up one way or another after she appears too late for the election.

"Just figure things out, George. Do you think Noonan got Mike the Goat to assess the girls on the row a dollar apiece for your flowers from the Young Men's Republican Club, for his health! You had the grace to thank Pat, but if you didn't know where they came from," explained Mr. Evans cynically, "it was because you have forgotten where all Pat's floral offerings from the Y. M. R. C. come from at weddings and funerals! And Pat feels that you're his kind of people.

"Politics, George, is not the chocolate éclair that you might think it, if you didn't know it! Use your bean, my boy! Use your bean! And you'll see why Pat Noonan lines up with the rugged captains of industry who are the bulwarks of our American liberty. Pat uses his head for something more than a hatrack."

The two puffed for a time in silence. Finally the host said: "Well, let's turn in."

Three minutes later George called across the upper hall to Penfield.

"The joke's on us, Penny. Here's a note saying that Genevieve is over with Betty for the night. We'll call her up after breakfast and have them both over to a surprise party."

Penny strolled across to his friend's door. He was disappointed, and he showed it. He found George sitting on the side of his bed.

"Penny," mused the Young Man in Politics, in his finest mood, "you know I sometimes think that, perhaps, way down deep, there is something wrong with our politics. I don't like to be hooked up with Noonan and his gang. And I don't like the way Noonan and his gang are hooked up with Wesley Norton and the silk stockings and Uncle Martin and the big fellows. Why can't we get rid of the Noonan influence? They aren't after the things we're after! They only furnish the unthinking votes that make majorities that elect the fellows the big crooks handle. Lord, man, it's a dirty mess! And why women want to get into the dirty mess is more than I can see."

"What a sweet valedictory address you are making for a young ladies' school!" scoffed Penny. "The hills are green far off! Aren't you the Sweet Young Thing. But I'll tell you why the women want to get in, George. They think they want to clean up the mess."

"But would they clean it? Wouldn't they vote about as we vote?"

" Well," answered Mr. Evans with the cynicism of the judicial mind, "let's see. You know now, if you didn't know at the time, that Noonan got Mike the Goat to assess the disorderly houses for the money to buy your wedding roses from the Y. M. R. C. All right. Noonan's bartender is on the ticket with you as assemblyman. Are you going to vote for him or not?"

"But, Penny, I've just about got to vote for him."

"All right, then. I'll tell Genevieve the truth about Noonan and the flowers, and I'll ask her if she would feel that she had to vote for Noonan's bartender!" retorted Mr. Evans. "Giving women the ballot will help at least that much. If the Noonans stay in politics, they'll get no help from the women when they vote!"

"But aren't we protecting the women?"

"Anyway, Mrs. Remington," said E. Eliot comfortably, "I'm glad it happened just this way. Without you, they would hold me until after the election on Tuesday. With you, about tomorrow at ten o'clock we shall be released. E. Eliot alone they have made every provision for holding. They have started a scandal, I don't doubt, necessary to explain my absence, and pulled the political wires to keep me from making a fuss about it afterward. They know their man in the district attorney's office, and—"

"Do you mean George Remington?" This from his wife, with flashing eyes.

"I mean," explained E. Eliot unabashed, "that for some reason they feel safe with George Remington in the district attorney's office, or they would not kidnap me to prevent his defeat! That is the cold-blooded situation."

"This party," E. Eliot smiled, "is given at the country home of Mike the Goat, as nearly as I can figure it out. Mike is a right-hand man of Noonan. Noonan is a right-hand man of Benjie Doolittle and Wesley Norton, and they are all a part of the system that holds Martin Jaffry's industries under the amiable beneficence of our sacred protective tariff! Hail, hail, the gang's all here—what do we care now, my dear? And because you are here and are part of the heaven-born combination for the public good, I am content to go through the rigors of one night without a nightie for the sake of the cause!"

"But they don't know who I am!" protested Mrs. Remington. "And—"

"Exactly, and for that reason they don't know who you are not. Tomorrow the whole town will be looking for you, and Noonan will hear who you are and where you are. Then! Say, girl—*say, girl,* it *will* be grist for our mill! Fancy the headlines all over the United States:

'GANG KIDNAPS CANDIDATE'S WIFE
Mystery Shrouds Plot
Candidate Remington is Silent.'"

"But he won't be silent," protested the indignant Genevieve. "I tell you, he'll denounce it from the platform. He'll never let this outrage—"

"Well, my dear," said the imperturbable E. Eliot, "when he denounces this plot he'll have to denounce Doolittle and Noonan, and probably Norton, and maybe his Uncle Martin Jaffry. Somebody is paying big money for this job! I said the headlines will declare:

'Candidate Remington is Silent

But Still Maintains That Women Are Protected
from Rigors of Cruel World by Man's
Chivalry.'"

"Oh, Miss Eliot, don't! How can you? Oh, I know George will not let this outrage—"

"Of course not," hooted E. Eliot. "The sturdy oak will support the clinging vine! But while he is doing it he will be defeated. And if he doesn't protest he will be defeated, for I shall talk!"

"George Remington will face defeat like a gentleman, Miss Eliot; have no fear of that. He will speak out, no matter what happens."

"And when he speaks, when he tells the truth about this whole alliance between the greedy, ruthless rich and the brutal, vicious dregs of this community—our cause is won!"

The next morning George Remington reached from his bed for his telephone and called up the Sheridan residence. Two minutes later Penfield Evans heard a shout. At his door stood the unclad and pallid candidate for district attorney.

"Penny," he gasped, "Genevieve's not there! She has not been with Betty all night. And Betty has gone out to find E. Eliot, who is missing from her boarding-house!"

"Are you sure—"

"God—Penny—I thought I had stopped it!"

George was back in his room, flying into his clothes. The two men were talking loudly. From down the hall a sleepy voice—unmistakably Mrs. Brewster-Smith's—was drawling:

"George—George—are you awake? I didn't hear you come in. Dear Genevieve went over to stay all night with Cousin Betty, and the oddest thing happened. About midnight the telephone bell rang, and that odious Eliot person called you up!"

George was in the hall in an instant and before Mrs. Brewster-Smith's door.

"Well, well, for God's sake, what did she say!" he cried.

"Oh, yes, I was coming to that. She said to send your chauffeur with the car down to the—oh, I forget, some nasty factory or something, for Genevieve. She said Genevieve was down there talking to the factory girls. Fancy that, George! So I just put up the receiver. I knew Genevieve was with Betty Sheridan and not with that odious person at all—it was some ruse to get your car and compromise you. Fancy dear Genevieve talking to the factory girls at midnight!"

Penfield Evans and George Remington, standing in the hall, listened to these words with terror in their hearts.

"Get Noonan first," said George. "I'll talk to him."

In five seconds Evans had Noonan's residence. Remington listened to Penny's voice.

"Gone," he was saying. "Gone where?" And then: "Why, he was at the dinner last—What's Doolittle's number?" ("Noonan went to New York on the midnight train," he threw at George.) A moment later Remington heard his partner cry, "Doolittle's gone to New York? On the midnight train?"

"Try Norton," snapped George. Soon he heard Penny exclaim. "Albany?" said Penny. "Mr. Norton is in Albany? Thank you!"

"Their alibis!" said Evans calmly, as he hung up the receiver and stared at his partner.

"Well, it—it—Why, Penny, they've stolen Genevieve! That damned Mike and the Armenian! They've got Genevieve with that Eliot woman! God—Why, Penny, for God's sake, what—"

"Slowly, George—slowly. Let's move carefully."

The voice of Penfield Evans was cool and steady.

"First of all, we need not worry about any harm coming to Genevieve. She is with Miss Eliot, and that woman has more sense than a man. She may be depended upon. Now, then," Evans waved his partner to silence and went on: "the next thing to consider is how much publicity we shall give this episode." He paused.

"It's not a matter of publicity; it's a matter of getting Genevieve immediately."

"An hour or so of publicity of the screaming, hysterical kind will not help us to find Genevieve. But when we do find her, our publicity will have defeated you!"

The two men stared at each other. Remington said: "You mean I must shield the organization!"

"If you are to be elected—yes!"

"Do you think Genevieve and Miss Eliot would consent to shield the organization when we find them? Why, Penny, you're mad! We must call up the chief of police! We must scour the country! I propose to go right to the newspapers! The more people who know of this dastardly thing the sooner we shall recover the victims!"

"And the sooner Noonan, when he comes home tonight, will denounce you as an accessory before the fact, with Norton and Doolittle as corroborating witnesses for him! Oh, you're learning politics fast, George!"

The thought of what Genevieve would say when she knew, through Noonan and Doolittle, that he had heard of the plot to kidnap Miss Eliot, and within an hour had talked to his wife casually at luncheon without saying anything about it, made George's heart stop. He realized that he was learning something more than politics. He walked the floor of the room.

"Well," he said at last, "let's call in Uncle Martin Jaffry. He—"

"Yes; he is probably paying for the job. He might know something! I'll get him."

"Paying for the job! Do you think he knew of this plot?" cried George as Evans stood at the telephone.

"Oh, no. He just knew, in a leer from Doolittle, that they had extraordinary need for five thousand dollars or so in your behalf—that they had consulted you. And then Doolittle winked and Noonan cocked his head rakishly, and Uncle Martin put—Hello, Mr. Jaffry. This is Penny. Dress and come down to the office quickly. We are in serious trouble."

Twenty minutes later Uncle Martin was sitting with the two young men in the office of Remington and Evans. When they explained the situation to him his dry little face screwed up.

"Well, at least Genevieve will be all right," he muttered. "E. Eliot will take care of her. But, boys—boys," he squeezed his hands and rocked in misery, "the devil of it is that I gave Doolittle the money in a check and then went and got another check from the Owners' Protective Association and took the peak load off myself, and Doolittle was with me when I got the P. A. check. We've simply got to protect him. And, of course, what he knows, Noonan knows. We can't go tearing up Jack here, calling police and raising the town!"

George Remington rose.

"Then I've got to let my wife lie in some dive with that unspeakable Turk and that Mike the Goat while you men dicker with the scoundrels who committed this crime!" he said. "My God, every minute is precious! We must act. Let me call the chief of police and the sheriff—"

"All dear friends of Noonan's," Penny quietly reminded him. "They probably have the same tip about what is on as you and

Uncle Martin have! Calm down, George! First, let me go out and learn when Noonan and Doolittle are coming home! When we know that, we can—"

"Penny, I can't wait. I must act now. I must denounce the whole damnable plot to the people of this country. I must not rest one second longer in silence as an accessory. I shall denounce—"

"Yes, George, you shall denounce," exclaimed his partner. "But just whom—yourself, that you did not warn Miss Eliot all day yesterday!"

"Yes," cried Remington, "first of all, myself as a coward!"

"All right. Next, then, your Uncle Martin Jaffry, who was earnestly trying to help you in the only way he knew how to help! Why, George, that would be—"

"That would be the least I could do to let the people see—"

"To let the people see that Mrs. Brewster-Smith and all your social friends in this town are associated with Mike the Goat and his gang—"

Before Evans could finish, his partner stopped him.

"Yes, yes—the whole damned system of greed! The rich greed and the poor greed—our criminal classes plotting to keep justice from the decent law-abiding people of the place, who are led like sheep to the slaughter. What did the owners pay that money for? Not for the dirty job that was turned—not primarily. But to elect me, because they thought I would not enforce the factory laws and the housing laws and would protect them in their larceny! That money Uncle Martin collected was my price—my price!"

He was standing before his friends, rigid and white in rage. Neither man answered him.

"And because the moral sense of the community was in the hearts and heads of the women of the community," he went on, "those who are upholding the immoral compact between business and politics had to attack the womanhood of the town—and Genevieve's peril is my share in the shame. By God, I'm through!"

XIII

BY MARY AUSTIN

CLOSE on Young Remington's groan of utter disillusionment came a sound from the street, formless and clumsy, but brought to a sharp climax with the crash of breaking glass.

Even through the closed window which Penfield Evans hastily threw up, there was an obvious quality to the disturbance which revealed its character even before they had grasped its import.

The street was still full of morning shadows, with here and there a dancing glimmer on the cobbles of the still level sun, caught on swinging dinner pails as the loosely assorted crowd drifted toward shop and factory.

In many of the windows half-drawn blinds marked where spruce window trimmers added last touches to masterpieces created overnight, but directly opposite nothing screened the offense of the Voiceless Speech, which continued to display its accusing questions to the passer-by.

Clean through the plate-glass front a stone had crashed, leaving a heap of shining splinters, on either side of which a score of men and boys loosely clustered, while further down a ripple of disturbance marked where the thrower of the stone had just vanished into some recognized port of safety.

It was a clumsy crowd, half-hearted, moved chiefly by a cruel delight in destruction for its own sake, and giving voice at intervals to coarse comment of which the wittiest penetrated through a stream of profanity, like one of those same splinters of glass, to the consciousness of at least two of the three men who hung listening in the window above:

"To hell with the——suffragists!"

At the same moment another stone hurled through the break sent the Voiceless Speech toppling; it lay crumpled in a pathetic feminine sort of heap, subject to ribald laughter, but Penny Evans' involuntary cry of protest was cut off by his partner's hand on his shoulder.

"They're Noonan's men, Penny; it's a put-up job."

George had marked some of the crowd at the meetings Noonan had arranged for him, and the last touch to the perfunctory character of the disturbance was added by the leisurely stroll of the policeman turning in at the head of the street. Before he reached the crowd it had redissolved into the rapidly filling thoroughfare.

"It's no use, Penny. Our women have seen the light and beaten us to it; we've got to go with them or with Noonan and his—Mike the Goat!"

Recollection of his wife's plight cut him like a knife. "The Brewster-Smith women have got to choose for themselves!" He felt about for his hat like a man blind with purpose.

The street sweeper was taking up the fragments of the shattered windows half an hour later, when Martin Jaffry found himself going rather aimlessly along Main Street with a feeling that the bottom had recently dropped out of things—a sensation which, if the truth must be told, was greatly augmented by the fact that he hadn't yet breakfasted.

He had remained behind the two younger men to get into communication with Betty Sheridan and ask her to stay close to the telephone in case Miss Eliot should again attempt to get into touch with her. He lingered still, dreading to go into any of the places where he was known lest he should somehow be led to commit himself embarrassingly on the subject of his nephew's candidacy.

His middle-aged jauntiness considerably awry, he moved slowly down the heedless street, subject to the most gloomy reflections. Like most men, Martin Jaffry had always been dimly aware that the fabric of society is held together by a system of mutual weaknesses and condonings, but he had always thought of himself and his own family as moving freely in the interstices, peculiarly exempt, under Providence, from strain. Now here they were, in such a position that the first stumbling foot might tighten them all into inextricable scandal.

It is true that Penny, at the last moment, had prevailed on

George to put off the relief of his feelings by public repudiation of his political connections, at least until after a conference with the police. And to George's fear that the newspapers would get the news from the police before he had had a chance to repudiate, he had countered with a suggestion, drawn from an item in the private history of the chief—known to him through his father's business—which he felt certain would quicken the chief's sense of the propriety of keeping George's predicament from the press.

"My God!" said George in amazement, and Martin Jaffry had responded fervently with "O Lord!"

Not because it shocked him to think that there might be indiscretions known to the lawyer of a chief of police which the chief might not wish known to the world, but because, with the addition of this new coil to his nephew's affairs, he was suddenly struck with the possibility of still other coils in any one of which the saving element of indiscretion might be wanting.

Suppose they should come upon one, just one impregnable honesty, one soul whom the fear of exposure left unshaken. On such a possibility rested the exemption of the Jaffry-Remingtons.

It was the reference to E. Eliot in his instructions to Betty which had awakened in Jaffry's mind the disquieting reflection that just here might prove such an impregnability. They probably wouldn't be able to "do anything" with E. Eliot simply because she herself had never done anything she was afraid to go to the public about. To do him justice, it never occurred to him that in the case of a lady it was easily possible to invent something which would be made to answer in place of an indiscretion.

Probably that was Martin Jaffry's own impregnability—that he wouldn't have lied about a lady to save himself. What he did conclude was that it was just this unbending quality of women, this failure to provide the saving weakness, which unfitted them for political life.

He shuddered, seeing the whole fabric of politics fall in ruins around an electorate composed largely of E. Eliots, feeling himself stripped of everything that had so far distinguished him from the Noonans and the Doolittles.

Out of his sudden need for reinstatement with himself, he

raised in his mind the vision of woman as the men of Martin
Jaffry's world conceived her—a tender, enveloping medium in
which male complacency, unchecked by any breath of criticism,
reaches its perfect flower—the flower whose fruit, eaten in secret
and afar from the soil which nourishes it, is graft, corruption and
civic incompetence.

Instinctively his need directed him toward the Remington
place.

Mrs. Brewster-Smith was glad to see him. Between George's
hurried departure and Jaffry's return several of the specters that
haunt such women's lives looked boldly in at the window.

There was the specter of scandal, as it touched the Remingtons,
touching that dearest purchase of femininity, social standing; there
was the specter of poverty, which threatened from the exposure of
the source of her income and the enforcement of the law; nearer
and quite as poignant, was the specter of an ignominious retreat
from the comfort of George Remington's house to her former
lodging, which she was shrewd enough to realize would follow
close on the return of her cousin's wife.

All morning she had beaten off the invisible host with that
courage—worthy of a better cause—with which women of her
class confront the assaults of reality; and the sight of Martin Jaffry
coming up the broad front walk met her like a warm waft of secu-
rity. She flung open the door and met him with just that mixture
of deference and relief which the situation demanded.

She was terribly anxious about poor Genevieve, of course, but
not so anxious that she couldn't perceive how Genevieve's poor
uncle had suffered.

"What, no breakfast! Oh, you *poor* man! Come right out into
the dining-room."

Mrs. Brewster-Smith might have her limitations, but she was
entirely aware of the appeasing effect of an open fire and a spread
cloth even when no meal is in sight; she was adept in the art of enveloping tenderness and the extent to which it may be augmented
by the pleasing aroma of ham and eggs and the coffee which she
made herself. And oh, those *poor* women, what *disaster* they were

bringing on themselves by their prying into things that were better left to more competent minds, and what pain to *other* minds! *So selfish,* but of course they didn't realize. Really she hoped it would be a *lesson* to Genevieve. The dear girl was so changed that she didn't see how she was going to go on living with her; though, of course, she would like to stand by dear George—and a woman did *so* appreciate a home!

At this point the enveloping tenderness of Mrs. Brewster-Smith concentrated in her fine eyes, just brushed the heart of her listener as with a passing wing, hovered a moment, and dropped demurely to the tablecloth.

In the meantime two sorely perplexed citizens were grappling with the problem of the disappearance of two highly respectable women from their homes under circumstances calculated to give the greatest anxiety to faithful "party" men. It hadn't needed Penny's professional acquaintance with Chief Buckley to impress the need of secrecy on that official's soul. "Squeal" on Noonan or Mike the Goat? Not if he knew himself. Naturally Mr. Remington must have his wife, but at the same time it was important to proceed regularly.

"And the day before election, too!" mourned the chief. "Lord, what a mess! But keep cool, Mr. Remington; this will come out all right!"

After half an hour of such ineptitudes, Penfield Evans found it necessary to withdraw his partner from the vicinity of the police before his impatience reached the homicidal pitch.

"Buckley's no such fool as he sounds," Penny advised. "He probably has a pretty good idea where the women are hidden, but you must give him time to tip off Mike for a getaway."

But the suggestion proved ill chosen, at least so far as it involved a hope of keeping George from the newspapers. Shocked to the core of his young egotism as he had been, Remington was yet not so shocked that the need of expression was not stronger in him than any more distant consideration.

"Getaway!" he frothed. "Getaway! While a woman like my wife—" But the bare idea was too much for him.

"They may get away, but they'll not get off—not a damned one of them—of *us,*" he corrected himself, and with face working the popular young candidate for district attorney set off almost on a run for the office of the *Sentinel.*

Reflecting that if his friend was bent upon official suicide, there was still no reason for his being a witness to it, Penny turned aside into a telephone booth and called up Betty Sheridan. He heard her jump at the sound of his voice, and the rising breath of relief running into his name.

"O-o-oh, Penny! Yes, about twenty minutes ago. Genevieve is with her. . . . Oh, yes, I'm sure."

Her voice sounded strong and confident.

"They're in a house about an hour from the factory," she went on, "among some trees. I'm sure she said trees. We were cut off. No, I couldn't get her again. . . . Yes . . . it's a party line. In the Redfield district. Oh, Penny, do you think they'll do her any harm?"

It was, no doubt, the length of time it took to assure Miss Sheridan on this point that prevented Evans from getting around to the *Sentinel,* whose editor was at that moment giving an excellent exhibition of indecision between his obligation as a journalist and his rôle of leading citizen in a town where he met his subscribers at dinner.

It was good stuff—oh, it was good! What headlines!

PROMINENT SOCIETY WOMEN
KIDNAPPED

Candidate Remington Repudiates Party!

It was good for a double evening edition. On the other hand, there was Norton, one of his largest advertisers. There was also the rival city of Hamilton, which was even now basely attempting to win away from Whitewater a recently offered Carnegie library on the ground of its superior fitness.

Finally there was the party.

The *Sentinel* had always been a sound party organ. But *what* a scoop! And suppose it were possible to save the party at the expense of its worst element? Suppose they raised the cry of reform and brought Remington in on a full tide of public indignation? Would Mike stand the gaff? If it were made worth his while. But what about Noonan and Doolittle? So the editorial mind shuttled to and fro amid the confused outpourings of the amazed young candidate, while with eyes bright and considering as a rat's the editor followed Remington in his pacings up and down the dusty, littered room.

Completely occupied with his own reactions, George's repudiation swept on in an angry, rapid stream which, as it spent itself, began to give place to the benumbing consciousness of a divided hearing.

Until this moment Remington had had a pleasant sense of the press as a fine instrument upon which he had played with increasing mastery, a trumpet upon which, as his mind filled with commendable purposes, he could blow a very pretty tune,—a noble tune with now and then a graceful flourish acceptable to the public ear. Now as he talked he began to be aware of flatness, of squeaking keys. . . .

"Naturally, Mr. Remington, I'll have to take this up with the business management . . ." dry-lipped, the tune sputtered out.

At this juncture the born journalist awaked again in the editorial breast at the entrance of Penfield Evans with his new item of Betty's interrupted message.

Two women shut up in a mysterious house among the trees! Oh, hot stuff, indeed!

Under it George rallied, recovered a little of the candidate's manner.

"Understand," he insisted. "This goes in even if I have to pay for it at advertising rates."

A swift pencil raced across the paper as Remington's partner swept him off again to the police.

Betty's call had come a few minutes before ten. What had happened was very simple.

The two women had been given breakfast, for which their hands had been momentarily freed. When the bonds had been tied

again it had been easy for E. Eliot to hold her hands in such a position that she was left, when their keeper withdrew, with a little
freedom of movement.

By backing up to the knob she had been able to open a door
into an adjoining room, in which she had been able to make out a
telephone on a stand against the wall.

This room also had locked windows and closed shutters, but
her quick wit had enabled her to make use of that telephone.

Shouldering the receiver out of the hook, she had called
Betty's number, and, with Genevieve stooping to listen at the dangling receiver, had called out two or three broken sentences.

Guarded as their voices had been, however, some one in the
house had been attracted by them, and the wire had been cut at
some point outside the room. E. Eliot and Genevieve came to this
conclusion after having lost Betty and failed to raise any answer to
their repeated calls. Somebody came and looked in at them
through the half-open door, and, seeing them still bound, had gone
away again with a short, contemptuous laugh.

"No matter," said E. Eliot. "Betty heard us, and the central
office will be able to trace the call."

It was because she could depend on Betty's intelligence, she
went on to say, that she had called her instead of the Remington
house—for suppose that fool Brewster-Smith woman had come to
the telephone!

She and Genevieve occupied themselves with their bonds,
fumbling back to back for a while, until Genevieve had a brilliant
idea. Kneeling, she bit at the cords which held Miss Eliot's wrists
until they began to give.

What Betty had done intelligently was nothing to what she
had done without meaning it. She had been unkind to Pudge.
Young Sheridan was in a condition which, according to his own
way of looking at it, demanded the utmost kindness.

Following a too free indulgence in *marrons glacés* he had been
relegated to a diet that reduced him to the extremity of despera-
tion.

Not only had he been forbidden to eat sweets, but while his

soul still longed for its accustomed solace, his stomach refused it, and he was unable to eat a box of candied fruit which he had with the greatest ingenuity secured.

And that was the occasion Betty took—herself full of nervous starts and mysterious recourse to the telephone behind locked doors—to remind him cruelly that he was getting flabby from staying too much in the house and to recommend a long walk for his good.

It was plain that she would stick at nothing to get her brother out of the way, and Pudge was cut to the heart.

Oh, well, he would go for a walk, from which he would probably be brought home a limp and helpless cripple. Come to think of it, if he once got started to walk he was not sure he would ever turn back; he would just walk on and on into a kinder environment than this.

After all, it is impossible to walk in that fateful way in a crowded city thoroughfare. Besides, one passes so many confectioners with their mingled temptation and disgust. Pudge rode on the trolley as far as the city limits. Here there was softer ground underfoot and a hint of melancholy in the fields. A flock of crows going over gave the appropriate note.

Off there to the left, set back from the road among dark, crowding trees, stood a mysterious house. Pudge always insisted that he had known it for mysterious at the first glance. It had a mansard roof and shutters of a sickly green, all closed; there was not a sign of life about, but smoke issued from one of the chimneys.

Here was an item potent to raise the sleuth that slumbers in every boy, even in such well-cushioned bosoms as Pudge Sheridan's.

He paused in his walk, fell into an elaborately careless slouch, and tacked across the open country toward the back of the house. Here he discovered a considerable yard fenced with high boards that had once been painted the same sickly green as the shutters, and a great buckeye tree just outside, spreading its branches over the corner furthest from the house.

Toward this post of observation he was drifting with that fine assumption of aimlessness which can be managed on occasion by almost any boy, when he was arrested by a slight but unmistakable shaking of one of the shutters, as though some one from within were trying the fastenings.

The shaking stopped after a moment, and then, one after another, the slats of the double leaves were seen to turn and close as though for a secret survey of the field. After a moment or two this performance was repeated at the next window on the left, and finally at a third.

Here the shaking was resumed after the survey, and ended with the shutter opening with a snap and being caught back from within and held cautiously on the crack. Pudge kicked clods in his path and was pretentiously occupied with a dead beetle which he had picked up.

All at once something flickered across the ground at his feet, swung two or three times, touched his shoe, traveled up the length of his trousers and rested on his breast. How that bosom leaped to the adventure!

He fished hurriedly in his pocket and brought up a small round mirror. It had still attached to its rim a bit of the ribbon by which it had been fastened to his sister's shopping bag, from which, if the truth must be told, he had surreptitiously detached it.

Pretending to consult it, as though it were some sort of pocket oracle, Pudge flashed back, and presently had the satisfaction of seeing a bright fleck of light travel across the shutter. Immediately there was a responsive flicker from the window: one, two, three, he counted, and flashed back: one, two, three.

Pudge's whole being was suffused with delicious thrills. He wished now he had obeyed that oft-experienced presentiment and learned the Morse code; it was a thing no man destined for adventure should be without. This wordless interchange went on for a few moments, and then a hand, a woman's hand—O fair, imprisoned ladies of all time!—appeared cautiously at the open shutter, waved and pointed.

It pointed toward the buckeye tree. Pudge threw a stone in that direction and sauntered after it, pitching and throwing. Once at the corner, after a suitable exhibition of casualness, he climbed until he found himself higher than the fence, facing the house.

While he was thus occupied, things had been happening there. The shutter had been thrown back and a woman was climbing down by the help of a window ledge below and a pair of knotted window curtains.

Another woman prepared to follow her, gesticulating forcibly to the other not to wait, but to run. Run she did, but it was not until Pudge, lying full length on the buckeye bough, reached her a hand that he discovered her to be his sister's friend, Genevieve Remington.

In the interval of her scrambling up by the aid of the bent bough and such help as he could give her, they had neglected to observe the other woman. Now, as Mrs. Remington's heels drummed on the outside of the fence, Pudge was aware of some commotion in the direction of the house, and saw Miss Eliot running toward him, crying: "Run, run!" while two men pursued her. She made a desperate jump toward the tree, caught the branch, hung for a moment, lost her hold, and brought Pudge ignominiously down in a heap beside her.

If Miss Eliot had not contradicted it, Pudge would have believed to his dying day that bullets hurtled through the air; it was so necessary to the dramatic character of the adventure that there should be bullets. He recovered from the shock of his fall in time to hear Miss Eliot say: "Better not touch me, Mike; if there's so much as a bruise when my friends find me, you'll get sent up for it."

Her cool, even tones cut the man's stream of profanity like a knife. He came threateningly close to her, but refrained from laying hands on either of them.

Meantime his companion drew himself up to the top of the fence for a look over, and dropped back with a gesture intended to be reassuring. Pudge rose gloriously to the occasion.

"The others have gone back to call the police," he announced. Mike spat out an oath at him, but it was easy to see that he was not at all sure that this might not be the case. The possibility that it might be, checked a movement to pursue the fleeing Genevieve. Miss Eliot caught their indecision with a flying shaft.

"Mrs. George Remington," she said, "will probably be in communication with her friends very shortly. And between his wife and his old and dear friend Mike it won't take George Remington long to choose."

This was so obvious that it left the men nothing to say. They fell in surlily on either side of her, and without any show of resistance she walked calmly back toward the house. Pudge lingered, uncertain of his cue.

"Beat it, you putty-face!" Mike snarled at him, showing a yellow fang. "If you ain't off the premises in about two shakes, you'll get what's comin' to you. See?"

Pudge walked with as much dignity as he could muster in the direction of the public road. He could see nothing of Mrs. Remington in either direction; now and then a private motor whizzed by, but there was no other house near enough to suggest a possibility of calling for help.

He concealed himself in a group of black locusts and waited. In about half an hour he heard a car coming from the house with the mansard roof, and saw that it held three occupants, two men and a woman. The men he recognized, and he was certain that the woman, though she was well bundled up, was not E. Eliot.

The motor turned away from the town and disappeared in the opposite direction. Pudge surmised that Mike was making his getaway. He waited another half hour and began to be assailed by the pangs of hunger. The house gave no sign; even the smoke from the chimney stopped.

He was sure Miss Eliot was still there; imagination pictured her weltering in her own gore. Between fear and curiosity and the saving hope that there might be food of some sort in the house, Pudge left his hiding place and began a stealthy approach.

He came to the low stoop and crept up to the closed front door. Hovering between fear and courage, he knocked. But there was no response. With growing boldness he tried the door. It was locked.

The rear door also was bolted; but, creeping on, he found a high side window that the keepers of this prison in their hasty flight had forgotten to close.

With the aid of an empty rain barrel, which he overturned and rolled into position, Pudge scrambled with much hard breathing through the window, and dropped into the kitchen. Here he listened; his ears could discern no sound. On tiptoe he crept through the rooms of the first floor—but came upon neither furtive enemy nor imprisoned friend. Up the narrow stairway he crept—peeped into three bedrooms—and finally opening the door of what was evidently a storeroom, he found the object of his search.

E. Eliot sat in an old splint-bottomed chair—gagged, arms tied behind her and to the chair's back, and her ankles tied to the chair's legs. In a moment Pudge had the knotted towel out of her mouth, and had cut her bonds. But quick though Pudge was, to her he seemed intolerably slow; just then E. Eliot was thinking of only one thing.

This was the final afternoon of the campaign and she was away out here, far from all the great things that might be going on.

She gave a single stretch of her cramped muscles as she rose.

"I know you—you're Betty Sheridan's brother—thanks," she said briskly. "What time is it?"

Pudge drew out his most esteemed possession, a watch which kept perfect time—except when it refused to keep any time at all.

"Three o'clock," he announced.

"Then our last demonstration is under way, and when I tell my story—" E. Eliot interrupted herself. "Come on—let's catch the trolley!"

With Pudge panting after her, she hurried downstairs, unbolted the door, and, running lightly on the balls of her feet, sped in the direction of the street car line.

XIV

BY LEROY SCOTT

In the meantime, concern and suspense and irruptive wrath had their chief abode in the inner room of Remington and Evans. George had received a request, through Penny Evans, from the chief of police to remain in his office, where he could be reached instantly if information concerning Genevieve were received, and where his help could instantly be secured were it required; and Penny had enlarged that request to the magnitude of a command and had stood by to see that it was obeyed, and himself to give assistance.

George had recognized the sense of the order, but he rebelled at the enforced inactivity. Where was Genevieve?—why wasn't he out doing something for her? He strode about the office, fuming, sick with the suspense and inaction of his rôle.

But Genevieve was not his unbroken concern. He was still afire with the high resentment which a few hours earlier had made him go striding into the office of the *Sentinel*. Fragments of his statement to the editor leaped into his mind; and as he strode up and down he repeated phrases silently, but with fierce emphasis of the soul.

Now and again he paused at his window and looked down into Main Street. Below him was a crowd that was growing in size and disorder: the last afternoon of any campaign in Whitewater was exciting enough; much more so were the final hours of this campaign that marked the first entrance of women into politics in Whitewater on a scale and with an organized energy that might affect the outcome of the morrow's voting.

Across the way, Mrs. Herrington, the fighting blood of five generations of patriots roused in her, had reinstated the Voiceless Speech within the plate glass window broken by the stones of that morning and was herself operating it; and, armed with banners, groups of women from the Woman's Club, the Municipal League and the Suffrage Society were marching up and down the street sidewalks.

It was their final demonstration, their last chance to assert the demands of good citizenship—and it had attracted hundreds of curious men, vote-owners, belonging to what, in such periods of political struggle, are referred to on platforms as "our better element."

Also drifting into Main Street were groups of voters of less prepossessing aspect—Noonan's men, George recognized them to be. These jeered and jostled the marching women and hooted the remarks of the Voiceless Speech—but the women, disregarding insults and attacks, went on with their silent campaigning. The feeling was high—and George could see, as Noonan's men kept drifting into Main Street, that feeling was growing higher.

Looking down, George felt an angered exultation. Well, his statement in the *Sentinel,* due upon the street almost any moment, would answer all these and give them something to think about!— a statement which would make an even greater stir than the declaration which he had issued those many weeks ago, when, fresh from his honeymoon, he had begun his campaign for the district attorneyship. These people below certainly had a jolt coming to them!

George's impatient and glowering meditations—the hour was then near four—were broken in upon by several interruptions, which came on him in quick succession, as though detonated by brief-interval time-fuses. The first was the entrance of that straw-haired misspeller of his letters who had succeeded Betty Sheridan as guardian of the outer office.

"Mr. Doolittle is here," she announced. "He says he wants to see you."

"You tell Mr. Doolittle *I* don't want to see *him!*" commanded the irritated George.

But Mr. Benjamin Doolittle was already seeing his candidate. As political boss of his party, he had little regard for such a formality as being announced to any person on whom he might call—so he had walked through the open door.

Across the way, Mrs. Herrington, the fighting blood of five generations
of patriots roused in her, had reinstated the Voiceless Speech.

"Well, what d'you want, Doolittle?" George demanded aggressively.

Mr. Doolittle's face wore that look of bland solicitude, that unobtrusive partnership in the misfortune of others, which had made him such an admirable prosperous officiant at the last rites of residents of Whitewater.

"I just wanted to ask you, George—" he was beginning in his soft, lily-of-the-valley voice, when the telephone on George's desk started ringing. George turned and reached for it, to find that Penny had already picked up the instrument.

"I'll answer it, George. . . . Hello . . . Mr. Remington is here, but is busy; I'll speak for him—I'm Mr. Evans. What—it's *you!* Where are you? . . . Stay where you are; I'll come right over for you in my car."

"Who was that?" demanded George.

"Genevieve," Penny said rapidly, seizing his hat, "and I'm going—"

"So am I!" exclaimed George.

"Not till we've had a little understanding," sharply put in Doolittle, blocking his way.

"Stay here, George," his partner snapped out—"she's perfectly safe—just a little out of breath—telephoned from a drug store over in the Redfield district. I'll have her back here in fifteen minutes." And out Penny dashed, slamming the door.

But perhaps it was the straw-haired successor of Betty Sheridan who really prevented George from plunging after his partner.

"You ordered the *Sentinel* sent up as soon as it was out," she said. "Here are six copies."

George seized the ink-damp papers, and as the straw-haired one walked out in rubber-heeled silence he turned savagely upon his campaign manager.

"Well, Doolittle?" he demanded.

"I just want to ask you, George—"

George exploded. "Oh, you just want to ask me! Well, everything you want to ask me is answered in that paper. Read it!"

Doolittle took the copy of the *Sentinel* which was thrust into his hands. George watched him with triumphant grimness, await-

ing the effect of the bomb about to explode in the other's face. Mr.
Doolittle unfolded the *Sentinel*—looked it slowly through—then
raised his eyes to George. His face seemed somewhat puzzled, but
otherwise it was overspread with that sympathetic concern which,
as much as his hearse and his folding-chairs, was a part of his professional equipment.

"Why, George. I don't just get what you're driving at."

Forgetting that he was holding several copies of the *Sentinel,*
George dropped them all upon the floor and seized the paper from
Mr. Doolittle. He glanced swiftly over the first page—and experienced the highest voltage shock of his young public career. Feverishly he skimmed the remaining pages. But of all that he had
poured out in the office of the *Sentinel,* not one word was in print.

Automatically clutching the paper in a hand that fell to his
side, he stared blankly at his campaign manager. Mr. Doolittle
gazed back with his air of sympathetic concern, bewildered questioning in his eyes. And for a space, despite the increasing uproar
down in the street, there was a most perfect silence in the inner
office of Remington and Evans.

Before either of the two men could speak, the door was violently flung open and Martin Jaffry appeared. His clothing was dis-
arranged, his manner agitated—in striking contrast to the dapper
and composed appearance usual to that middle-aged little gentleman.

"George," he panted, "heard anything about Genevieve?"

"She's safe. Penny's got charge of her by this time."

His answer was almost mechanical.

"Thank God!" Uncle Martin collapsed in one of the office
chairs. "Mind—if sit here minute—get my breath."

George did not reply, for he had not heard. He was gazing
steadily at Mr. Doolittle; some great, but as yet shapeless, force was
surging up dazingly within him. But he somehow held himself in
control.

"Well, Doolittle," he demanded, "you said you came to ask
something."

Mr. Doolittle's manner was still propitiatingly bland. "I'll mention something else first, George, if you don't mind. You just re-

marked I'd find your answer in the *Sentinel*. There must 'a' been some little slip-up somewhere. So I guess I better mention first that the *Sentinel* has arranged to stand ready to get out an extra."

"An extra! What for?"

"Principally, George, I reckon to print those answers you just spoke of."

George still kept that mounting something under his control. "Answers to what?"

"Why, George," the other replied softly, persuasively. "I guess we'd better have a little chat—as man to man—about politics. Meaning no offense, George, stalling is all right in politics—but this time you've carried this stalling act a little too far. As the result of your tactics, George, why here's all this disorder in our streets—and the afternoon before election. If you'd only really tried to stop these messing women—"

"I didn't try to stop them by kidnapping them!" burst from George—and Uncle Martin, his breath recovered, now sat up, clutching his homespun cap.

"Kidnapping women?" queried the bland, bewildered voice of the party boss. "I say, George, I don't know what you're talking about."

"Why, you—" But George caught himself. "Speak it out, Doolittle—what do you want?"

"Since you ask it so frankly, George, I'll try to put it plain: You been going along handing out high-sounding generalities. There's nothing better and safer than generalities—usually. But this ain't no usual case, George. These women, stirring everything up, have got the solid interests so unsettled that they don't know where they're at—or where you're at. And a lot of boys in the organization feel the same way. What the crisis needs, George, is a plain statement of your intentions as district attorney, which we can get into that *Sentinel* extra and which will reassure the public—and the organization."

"A plain statement?" There was a grim set to George's jaw.

"Oh, it needn't go into too many details. Just what you might call a ringing declaration about this being the greatest era of prosperity Whitewater has ever known, and that you conceive it to be the duty of your administration to protect and stimulate this prosperity. The people will understand, and the organization will understand. I guess you get what I mean, George."

"Yes, I get what you mean!" exploded George, his fist crashing upon the table. "You mean you want me to be a complacent accessory to all the legal evasions that you and your political gang and the rich bunch behind you may want to get away with! You want me to be a crook in office! By God, Doolittle—"

"Shut up, Remington," snapped the political boss, his soft manner now vanished, his whole aspect now grimly menacing. "I know the rest of what you're going to say. I was pretty certain what it 'ud be before I came here, but I had to know for sure. Well, I know now, all right!"

His lank jaws snapped again.

"Since you are not going to represent the people that put you up, I demand your written withdrawal as candidate for the district attorney's office."

"And I refuse to give it!" cried George. "I was nominated by a convention, not by you. And I don't believe the party is as crooked as you—anyhow I'm going to give the decent members of the party a chance to vote decently! And you can't remove me from the ballot, either, for the ballot is already printed and—"

"That'll do you no—"

"I thought some time ago I was through with this political mess," George drove on. "But, Doolittle, damn you, I've just begun to get in it! And I'm going to see it through to the finish!"

Suddenly a thin little figure thrust itself between the bellicose pair and began shaking George's hand. It was Martin Jaffry.

"George—I guess I'm my share of an old scoundrel—and a trimmer—but hearing some one stand up and talk man's talk—" He broke off to shake George's hand again. "I thought you were the king of boobs—but, boy, I'm with you to wherever you want to go—if my money will last that far!"

"Keep out of this, Jaffry," roughly growled Doolittle. "It's too late for your dough to help this young pup. Remington, we may not take you off the ballot, but the organization kin send out word to the boys—"

"To knife me! Of course, I expect that! All right—go to it! But I'm on the ballot—you can't deprive people of the chance of voting for me. And I shall announce myself an independent and shall run as one!"

"We may not be able to elect our own nominee," harshly continued Doolittle, "but we kin send out word to back the Democratic candidate. Miller ain't much, but, at least, he's a soft man. And that *Sentinel* extra is going to say that a feeling has spread among the respectable element that it has lost confidence in you, and is going to say that prominent party members feel the party has made a mistake in ever putting you up. So run, damn you—run as a Democrat, a Republican, an Independent—but how are you going to git it across to the public in a way to do yourself any good—without backing? How are you going to git it across to the public?"

His last words, flung out with overmastering fury, brought George up short, and he saw this. Doolittle's wrath had mounted to that pitch which should never be reached by the resentment of a practical politician; it had attained such force that it drove him on to taunt his man.

"How are you going to git it before the public?" he again demanded, eyes agleam with triumphant rancor—"with us shutting you off and hammering you on one side?—and them damned messy women across the street hammering you from the other side? Oh, it's a grand chance you have—one little old grand chance! Especially with those dear damned females loving you like they do! Jest take a look at what the bunch over there are doing to you!"

Doolittle followed his own taunting suggestion; and George, too, glanced through his window across the crowded street into the shattered window whence issued the Voiceless Speech. In that jagged frame in the raw November air still stood Mrs. Harvey Herrington, turning the giant leaves of her soundless oratory. The heckling request which then struck George's eyes began: *"Will Candidate Remington answer—"*

George Remington read no more. His already tense figure suddenly stiffened; he caught a sharp breath. Then, without a word to the two men with him, be seized his hat and dashed from his office.

The street was even more a turbulent human sea, with violently twisting eddies, than had appeared from George's windows. It seemed that every member of the organizations whom Mrs. Herrington (and also Betty Sheridan, and later E. Eliot, and, at the last, Genevieve) had brought into this fight, were now downtown for the supreme effort. And it seemed that there were now more of the so-called "better citizens." Certainly there were more of Noonan's men, and these were still elbowing and jostling, and making little mass rushes—yet otherwise holding themselves ominously in control.

Into this milling assemblage George flung himself, so dominated by the fiery urge within him that he did not hear Genevieve call to him from Penny's car, which just then swung around the corner and came to a sharp stop on the skirts of the crowd. George shouldered his way irresistibly through this mass; the methods of his football days when he had been famed as a line-plunging back instinctively returned—and, all the fine chivalry forgotten which had given to his initial statement to the voters of Whitewater so noble a sound, he battered aside many of those "fairest flowers of our civilization, to protect whom it is man's duty and inspiration."

His lunging progress followed by curses and startled cries of feminine indignation, he at length emerged upon the opposite sidewalk, and, breathless and disheveled, he burst into the headquarters of the Voiceless Speech.

Some half-dozen of Mrs. Herrington's assistants cried out at his abrupt entrance. Mrs. Herrington, forward beside the speech, turned quickly about.

"Mr. Remington, you here!" she cried in amazement as he strode toward her. "What—what do you want?"

"I want—I want—" gasped George. But instead of finishing his sentence he elbowed Mrs. Herrington out of the way, shoved past her, and stepped forth in front of the Voiceless Speech. There, standing in the frame of jagged plate-glass, upon what was equivalent to a platform raised above the crowd, he sent forth a speech which had a voice.

"Ladies and gentlemen!" he called, raising an imperative hand. The uproar subsided to numerous exclamations, then to surprised silence; even Noonan's men checked their disorder at this appearance of their party's candidate.

"Ladies and gentlemen," and this Voiceful Speech was loud,—"I'm here to answer the questions of this contrivance behind me. But first let me tell you that though I'm on the ballot as the candidate of the Republican party, I do not want the backing of the Republican machine. I'm running as an Independent, and I shall act as an Independent.

"Here are my answers:

"I want to tell you that I shall enforce all the factory laws.

"I want to tell you that I shall enforce the laws governing housing conditions—particularly housing conditions in the factory district.

"I want to tell you that I shall enforce the laws governing child labor and the laws governing the labor of women.

"And I want to tell you that I shall enforce every other law, and shall try to secure the passage of further laws, which will make Whitewater a clean, forward-looking city, whose first consideration shall be the welfare of all.

"And, ladies and gentlemen—" he shouted, for the hushed voices had begun to rise—"I wish I could address you all as fellow-voters!—I want to tell you that I take back that foolish statement I made at the opening of the campaign.

"I want to tell you that I stand for, and shall fight for, equal suffrage!

"And I want to tell you that what has brought this change is what some of the women of Whitewater have shown me—and also some of the things our men politicians have done—our Doolittles, our Noonans—"

But George's speech terminated right there. Noise there had been before; now there burst out an uproar, and there came an artillery attack of eggs, vegetables, stones and bricks. One of the bricks struck George on the shoulder and drove him staggering back against the Voiceless Speech, sending that instrument of silent argument crashing to the floor. Regaining his balance, George started furiously back for the window; but Mrs. Herrington caught his arm.

"Let me go!" he called, trying to shake her off.

But she held on. "Don't—you've said enough!" she cried, and pulled him toward the rear of the room. "Look!"

Through the window was coming a heavier fire of impromptu grenades that rolled, spent, at their feet. But what they saw without was far more stirring and important. Noonan's men in the crowd, their hoodlumism now unleashed, were bowling over the people about them; but these really constituted Noonan's outposts and advance guards.

From out of two side streets, though George and Mrs. Herrington could not see their first appearance upon the scene, Noonan's real army now came charging into Main Street, as per that gentleman's grim instructions to "show them messin' women what it means to mess in politics." Hundreds of Whitewater's women were flung about, many sent sprawling to the pavement, and some hundreds of the city's most respectable voters, caught unawares, were hustled about and knocked down by the same ruthless drive.

"My God!" cried George, impulsively starting forward. "The damned brutes!"

But Mrs. Herrington still held his arm. "Come on—they're making a drive for this office!" breathlessly cried the quick-minded lady. "You can do no good here. Out the rear way—my car's waiting in the back street."

Still clutching his sleeve, Mrs. Herrington opened a door and ran across the back yard of McMonigal's building in a manner which indicated that that lady had not spent her college years (and similarly spent the years since then) propped among embroidered cushions consuming marshmallows and fudge.

The lot crossed, she hurried through a little grocery and thence into the street. Here they ran into a party that, seeing the riot on Main Street and the drive upon the window from which George had spoken, had rushed up reinforcements from the rear—a party consisting of Penny, E. Eliot, Betty Sheridan and Genevieve.

"Genevieve!" cried George, and caught her into his arms.

"Oh, George," she choked. "I—I heard it all—and it—it was simply wonderful!"

"George," cried Betty Sheridan, "I always knew, if you got the right kind of a jolt, you'd be—you'd be what you are!"

E. Eliot gripped his hand in a clasp almost as strong as George's arm. "Mr. Remington, if I were a man, I'd like to have the same sort of stuff in me."

"George, you old roughneck—" began Penny.

"George," interrupted Genevieve, still chokingly, her protective, wifely instinct now at the fore, "I saw you hit, and we're going to take you straight home—"

"Cut it all out," interrupted the cultured Mrs. Herrington. "This isn't Mr. Remington's honeymoon—nor his college reunion—nor the annual convention of his maiden aunts. This is Mr. Remington's campaign, and I'm his new campaign manager. And his campaign manager says he's not going away out to his home on Sheridan Road. His campaign headquarters are going to be in the center of town, at the Commercial Hotel, where he can be reached—for there's quick work ahead of us. Come on."

Five minutes later they were all in the Commercial Hotel's best suite.

"Now, to business, Mr. Remington," briskly began Mrs. Herrington. "Of course, that was a good speech. But why, in heaven's name, didn't you come out with it before?"

"I guess I really didn't know where I stood until today," confessed George, "and today I tried to come out with it."

And George went on to recount his experience with the *Sentinel*—his scene with Doolittle—and Doolittle's plan for an extra of the *Sentinel,* which was doubtless then in preparation.

"So they've got the *Sentinel* muzzled, have they—and are going to get out an extra repudiating you," Mrs. Herrington repeated. There came a flash into her quick, dark eyes. "I want our candidate to stay right here—rest up—get his thoughts in order. There are a lot of things to be done. I'll be back in an hour, Mr. Remington. The rest of you come along—you, too, Mrs. Remington."

Mrs. Herrington did not altogether keep her word in the matter of time. It was two hours before she was back. To George she handed a bundle of papers, remarking: "Thought you'd like to see that *Sentinel* extra."

"I suppose Doolittle has done his worst," he remarked grimly. He glanced at the paper. His face went loose with bewilderment at what he saw—headlines, big black headlines, bigger and blacker than he had ever before seen in the politically and typographically conservative *Sentinel*. He read through a few lines of print, then looked up.

"Why, it's all here!" he gasped. "The kidnapping of Miss Eliot and Genevieve by Noonan's men—my break with Doolittle, my denunciation of the party's methods, my coming out as an independent candidate—that riot on Main Street! How on earth did that ever get into the *Sentinel?*"

"Some straight talk, and quick talk, and the exercise of a little of the art of pressure they say you men exercise," was the prompt reply.

"I telephoned Mr. Ledbetter of the *Sentinel* advising him to hold the extra Mr. Doolittle had threatened until he heard from Mr. Wesley Norton, proprietor of the Norton Dry Goods Store. You know, Mr. Norton is the *Sentinel's* largest single advertiser and president of the Whitewater Business Men's Club.

"Then a committee of us women called on Mr. Norton and told him that we'd organize the women of the city and would carry on a boycott campaign against his store—we didn't really put it quite as crudely as that—unless he'd force the *Sentinel* to stop Mr. Doolittle's lying extra and print your statement.

"Mr. Norton gave in, and telephoned the *Sentinel* that if it didn't do as he said he'd cancel his advertising contract. Then, to make sure, we got hold of Mr. Jaffry, called on Mr. Ledbetter, who called in the business manager—and your Uncle Martin told them that unless they printed the truth, and every bit of it, and printed it at once, he was going to put up the money to start an opposition paper that *would print the truth*. That explains the extra."

"Well," ejaculated George, still staring, "you certainly are a wonder as a campaign manager!"

"Oh, I only did my fraction. That Miss Eliot did as much as I— she's a find—she's going to be one of Whitewater's really big women. And Betty Sheridan, you can't guess how Betty's worked —and your wife, Mr. Remington, she's turning out to be a marvel!

"But that's not all," Mrs. Herrington continued rapidly. "We bought ten thousand copies of that extra for ourselves—your uncle paid for them—and we're going to distribute them in every home in town. When the best element in Whitewater read how the women were trampled down by Noonan's mob—well, they'll know how to vote! Mr. Noonan will never guess how much he has helped us."

"You seem to have left nothing for me to do," said George.

"You'll find out there'll be all you'll want," replied the brisk Mrs. Herrington. "We're organizing meetings—one in every hall in the city, one on almost every other street corner, and we're going to rush you from one to the next—most of the night—and there'll be no letup for you tomorrow, even if it is election day. Yes, you'll find there'll be plenty to do!"

The next twenty-four hours were the busiest that George Remington had ever known in his twenty-six years.

But at nine o'clock the next evening it was over—the tumult and the shouting and the congratulations—and all were gone save only Martin Jaffry; and District-Attorney-Elect Remington sat in his hotel suite alone in the bosom of his family.

He was still dazed by what had happened to him—at the part he had unexpectedly played—dazed by the intense but well-ordered activity of the women: their management of his whirlwind tour of the city; their organization of parades with amazing swiftness; their rapid and complete house-to-house canvass—the work of Mrs. Herrington, of Betty, of that Miss Eliot, of hundreds of women—and especially of Genevieve.

He marveled especially at Genevieve because he had never thought of Genevieve as doing such things. But she *had* done them—he felt that somehow she was a different Genevieve: he didn't know what the difference was—he was in too much of a whirl for analysis—but he had an undefined sense of *aliveness,* of a spirited, joyous initiative in her.

She and all the rest seemed so strange as to be unbelievable. And yet, she—and all of it—true! . . .

From dramatic events and intangible qualities of the spirit, his consciousness shifted to material things—his immediate surroundings. Not till this blessed moment of relaxation did he become aware of the discomforts of this suite—nor did Genevieve fully appreciate the flamboyantly flowered maroon wall-paper and the jigsaw furniture.

"George," she sighed, "now that you're not needed down here, can't we go home?"

"Home!" The word came out half snort, half growl—hardly the tone becoming one whose triumph was so exultingly fresh. With a jar he had come back to a present which he fully understood. "Damn home! I haven't any home!"

Genevieve stared. Uncle Martin snickered, for Uncle Martin had the gift of understanding.

"You mean those flowers of womanhood whom chivalrous man—"

"Shut up," commanded George. He thought for a brief space; then his jaw set. "Excuse me a moment."

Drawing hotel stationery toward him, he scribbled rapidly and then sealed and addressed what he had written.

"Uncle Martin, your car's outside doing nothing; would you mind going on ahead and giving this little note to Cousin Alys Brewster-Smith, and then staying around and having a little supper with Genevieve and me? We'll be out soon, but there are a few things I want to talk over with Genevieve alone before we come."

Uncle Martin would oblige. But when he had gone, there seemed to be nothing of pressing importance that George had to communicate to Genevieve. Nor half an hour later, when he led his bride of four months up to their home, had he delivered himself of anything which seemed to require privacy.

As they stepped up on the porch, softly lighted by a frosted bulb in its ceiling, Cousin Emelene, her cat under her arm, came out of the front door and hurried past them, without speech.

"Why, Cousin Emelene!" George called after her.

She paused and half turned.

"You—you—" she half choked upon expletives that would not come forth. "The man will come for my trunks in the morning." Thrusting a handkerchief to her face, she hurried away.

"George, what can have happened to her?" cried the amazed Genevieve.

But George was saved answering her just then. Another figure had emerged from the front door—a rather largish figure, all in black—her left hand clutching the right hand of a child, aged, possibly, five. And this figure did not cower and hurry away. This figure halted, and glowered.

"George Remington," exclaimed Cousin Alys, "after your invitation—you—you apostate to chivalry! That outrageous letter! But if I am leaving your home, thank God I'm leaving it for a home of my own! Come on, Martin!"

With that she stalked away, dragging the sleepy Eleanor.

Not till then did George and Genevieve become aware that Uncle Martin was before them, having until now been obscured by Mrs. Brewster-Smith's outraged amplitude. His arms were loaded with coats, obviously feminine.

"Uncle Martin!" exclaimed George.

"George," gulped his uncle— "George—"And then he gained control of a dazed sort of speech. "When I gave her that letter I didn't know it was a letter of eviction. And the way she broke down before me—a woman, you know—I—I—well, George, it's my home she's going to."

"You don't mean—"

"Yes, George, that's just what I mean. Though, of course, I'm taking her back now to Mrs. Gallup's boarding-house until—until—good-night, George; good-night, Genevieve."

The little man went staggering down the walk with his burden of wraps; and after a minute there came the sound of his six-cylinder roadster buzzing away into the darkness.

"I didn't tell 'em they had to go tonight," said George doggedly. "But I did remark that even if every woman had a right to a home, every woman didn't have the right to make my home her home. Anyhow," his tone becoming softer, "I've at last got a home of my own. Our own," he corrected.

He took her in his arms. "And, sweetheart—it's a better home than when we first came to it, for now I've got more sense. Now it is a home in which each of us has the right to think and be what we please."

At just about this same hour just about this same scene was being enacted upon another front porch in Whitewater—there

being the slight difference that this second porch was not softly il-
luminated by any frosted globule of incandescence. Up the three
steps leading to this second porch Mr. Penfield Evans had that moment escorted Miss Elizabeth Sheridan.

"Good-night, Penny," she said.

He caught her by her two shoulders.

"See here, Betty—the last twenty-four hours have been
mighty busy hours—too busy even to talk about ourselves. But
now—see here, you're not going to get away with any rough work
like that. Come across, now. Will you?"

"Will I what?"

"Say, how long do you think you're a paid-up subscriber to this
little daily speech of mine? . . . Well, if I've got to hand you another copy, here goes. You promised me, on your word of honor, if
George swung around for suffrage, you'd swing around for me.
Well, George has come around. Not that I had much to do with
it—but he surely did come around! Now, the point is, Miss Betty
Sheridan, are you a woman of your promise—are you going to
marry me?"

"Well, if you try to put it that way, demanding your pound of
flesh—"

"One hundred and twenty pounds," corrected Penny.

"I'll say that, of course, I don't love you, but I guess a promise
is a promise—and—and—" And suddenly a pair of strong young
arms were flung about the neck of Mr. Penfield Evans. "Oh, I'm so
happy, Penny dear!"

"Betty!"

After that there was a long silence . . . silence broken only
by that softly sibilant detonation which belongs most properly to
the month of June, but confines itself to no season . . . to a long,
long silence born of and blessed by the gods . . . until one Percival Sheridan, coming stealthily home from a late debauch at
Humphrey's drug store, and mounting the steps in the tennis
sneakers which were his invariable wear on dry and non-state oc-
casions, bumped into the invisible and unhearing couple.

"Say, there—" gasped the startled youth, backing away.

Betty gave an affrighted cry—it was a long swift journey down from where she had just been. Her right hand, reaching drowningly out, fell upon a familiar shoulder.

"It's Pudge!" she cried. "Pudge"—shaking him—"snooping around, listening and trying to spy—"

"You stop that—it ain't so!" protested the outraged Pudge, his utterance throttled down somewhat by the chocolate cream in his mouth.

"Spying on people! And, besides, you've been stuffing yourself with candy again! You're ruining your stomach with that sticky sweet stuff—you're headed straight for a candy-fiend's grave. Now, you go upstairs and to bed!"

She jerked him toward the door, opened it, and as he was thrust through the door Pudge felt something, something warm, press impulsively against a cheek. Not until the door had closed upon him did he realize what Betty had done to him. He stood dazed for a moment—unbalanced between impulses. Then the sturdy maleness of fourteen rewon its dominance.

"Guess I know what they was doing, all right—aw, wouldn't it make you sick!" And, in disgust which another chocolate cream alleviated hardly at all, he mounted to his bed.

Outside there was again silence . . . faintly disturbed only by that softly sibilant, almost muted percussion which recalls inevitably the month of June. . . .

THE END